E

Margaret Meyers

BRANCHING OUT

BRANCHING OUT

•

GAIL HAMILTON

AVALON BOOKS
THOMAS BOUREGY AND COMPANY, INC.
401 LAFAYETTE STREET
NEW YORK, NEW YORK 10003

PRINTED IN THE UNITED STATES OF AMERICA
ON ACID-FREE PAPER
BY HADDON CRAFTSMEN, SCRANTON, PENNSYLVANIA

BRANCHING OUT

Chapter One

Oh, spring, thought Letty in anticipation as she struggled from the elevator in the lunchtime crowd. That very morning the season had turned. A warm wind had danced around her, tugging her hair, shaking the trees inside their iron grilles. A bright, renegade wind teasing with the wild scent of Lake Ontario so near the busy Toronto streets. A restless wind that had brought a lift of joy and an indefinable yearning even to Letty Smith's unpretentious heart. She meant to escape the office building and spend her lunch hour in the new green of the park.

As the mob streamed toward the front door, Letty peeled sideways into the annex for a shortcut she knew—only to find a yellow construction barrier blocking her way.

"Drat!"

There'd been notices about the renovations for weeks, but Letty, like every other employee in Bandis Towers, paid no attention until she found her path actually cut off

1

by a wooden trestle. The doors of all the offices beyond gaped open, their interiors emptied, their inhabitants shifted to other quarters, leaving only debris scattered in their wake. A splendid piece of art deco that part of the building was said to be, crying out for refurbishing to its original state. Some dramatic new life as a mini-mall was planned in conjunction with Letty's company, which did property management.

Ordinarily the soul of compliance, Letty was about to take the long way after all when she spotted it—the mere edge of a plastic pot dangling askew from one of the ceilings. The sides were streaked with dust. Brown strands drooped over the rim like scraggly, beseeching fingers, the ruin of what had once been a luxuriant spider plant.

Oh no!

Though hating to defy authority of any kind, Letty slipped round the barrier, heading for the pathetic scene. She could no more have ignored the abandoned plant than she could have walked past a drowning child, deaf to its cries for help.

Letty's weakness was a tender heart. She could not resist the sight of a shred of green struggling for its life and doomed to lose. And there were plenty of losers in a large office tower where people moved, quit, were transferred, got tired of their greenery or simply neglected it until there was nothing to do but pitch out the shriveled remains. All unintentionally, Letty had acquired a certain fame throughout the building. It consisted of, ''Hey, don't throw out that plant! There's some girl up on tenth will take it in.''

Letty had started innocently enough a week after her arrival by picking up a philodendron headed for oblivion on the trash trolley. Thinking no one noticed, she followed that by rescuing a painfully blistered African violet left to fry in the sun. Next came an Easter lily that had bloomed its heart out then keeled over in its pot. By osmosis, the word spread. The far-ranging mail staff became instrumental in bringing the drooping, withered orphans to Letty's desk. Finding homes for the convalescents was harder than trying to give away one-eyed kittens or old Christmas catalogs, making Letty run as fast as she could to keep ahead of the green tide. She rued the day she had become plant-mother to a minor skyscraper, but once started, she had no idea how to stop. Besides, she still got a thrill out of pouring that first drink into parching soil and practically hearing the astonished roots cry out, "Oh boy! Water! Give that lady a cheer!"

Now some hard-hearted wretch had moved on to cushy new digs without a thought for the helpless plant left to die behind. Letty considered the problem of detaching the pot from the ceiling hook high above her head. Too high for the owner to bother with watering, she supposed. Spotting a tipped-over swivel chair, Letty righted it and dragged it over even though two of its casters were missing and it tilted like a drunk on a binge. A tattered telephone book applied to the seat still did not give enough height, so Letty scrounged up a dented metal wastebasket, which she up-ended on top.

Gingerly, taking care to keep one hand on the wall, Letty clambered up this precarious edifice. By standing tiptoe on the wastebasket and stretching to the limit of her five-foot-five frame, she managed to get her fingers over the rim of the pot, where matters were exactly as expected.

"Dry as a banker's curse! Poor baby. We'll have you down in a flash."

Letty talked sagely, comfortingly, confidingly to plants, but only when strictly alone.

By dint of a little hop, Letty managed to free the pot from its hook. Unfortunately, the jolt also freed the frozen chair seat. To her horror, Letty felt it begin to swivel under her, twisting her away from the steadying nearness of the wall. The wastebasket began to slide toward the edge of the phone book and the phone book began to slide toward the edge of the chair. Everything went into slow motion for Letty as these items parted company beneath her feet. Dimly, as she fell, she thought she heard a shout punctuating a wild flurry of footsteps. An endless second later, she slammed straight into . . . a pillar?

No, couldn't be.

Pillars didn't clamp two strong arms around you and keep you from cracking your skull on the tiles. Interrupted momentum snapped Letty hard against what she instantly knew was a solid chest and equally solid thighs. The hanging pot continued to the floor, where it spun like a demented top on its plastic underside.

"Oooooffff!"

Her rescuer shuddered slightly from the force of her fall, but kept the rest of her upright as her feet thudded down. She wasn't released even when her legs quit wobbling and took her weight.

"If you're trying to break your neck, you need more altitude than that," commented a pained male voice after the first explosion of warm breath beside Letty's ear. "You'd have better luck if you went up two floors and jumped from the window ledge."

The arms held on tightly for a moment, then let go enough for Letty to spin round. She found herself nose to chest with a man wearing a jauntily tilted construction helmet, a red-checked work shirt, and a face caught up sternly into a frown. He kept hold of Letty's elbow.

"Didn't hurt yourself, did you?"

"N-n . . . no," Letty managed, afraid the fellow was going to yell at her for being in a construction area. If she'd been injured, why the fuss over insurance alone? . . .

"What's your name?"

"I . . . it doesn't matter. I'm nobody important. Just . . . ah, passing through." She pushed her hair from her eyes. "You're not going to . . . report me, are you?"

Tidy and orderly to her bones, Letty hated above all the fuss created by any breach of rules. This trait made her perfect for her job at Bandis Property Management, where it fell to her to untangle all discrepancies in the monthly rent collections.

Her captor leaned back on his heels, considering the wide-eyed scrap of female in a now disheveled wheaten pantsuit.

"I ought to," he returned severely, but now with just a hint of a twitch at the corner of his mouth. A wide, lean mouth it was, that could look firm very effectively.

Her heart still racketing around in her chest from the fall, Letty tried to read him and found herself unable to predict. He was what her mother would have called a big long drink of water, more than tall enough to look down a slightly crooked nose on Letty from his height.

And he had too much hair, she thought, curling from under the helmet, walnut brown and liberally streaked by the sun. The sun had got to his face too, putting it somewhere between tan and sunburned. But by far his most distinctive feature in the midst of all this was a set of amber eyes, so pale in color as to give him the look of a very inquisitive timber wolf.

"It all depends," he continued slowly, "on your explanation for climbing on that chair."

Letty pointed to the pot now come to rest practically against her ankle.

"Somebody had to save it before the wrecking crew gets here."

Disbelieving brows shot up.

"All that trouble over a dead plant?"

"It's not dead. Just thirsty. With a little water it'll . . ."

She stopped. He still hadn't let go of her elbow. His hand was warm and big and held her very easily.

"You could get a much nicer one, all green and bushy, at the Mart across the street."

"That's not the point," Letty asserted, beginning to re-cover her spirit. "It's this one that needs the help. If it gets some care, it'll soon be green and bushy too. It's a crying shame, people throwing out live plants just because they're tired of looking after them. Like . . . like throwing out a baby because you can't be bothered feeding it anymore!"

Letty had been through this argument countless times since she had started taking in plants. It was the one topic guaranteed to get her blood up. Without even thinking, she launched into a tirade at all the cruel and thoughtless things people did to their innocent greenery. Only after she had gotten all the way to her "faithful leafy companion" speech did she manage to catch herself.

"If it's too much trouble to take care of something, a person shouldn't have it in the first place!" she finished, dropping into a recalcitrant mumble.

"Indeed."

The amber eyes had sharpened from a hint of incipient mirth, and were now examining Letty intently. Something like surprise or intrigued pleasure flared in their depths.

"Indeed!" Letty echoed, picking up the pot and begin-ning to sidle back toward the breached barrier.

Her rescuer remained motionless, oblivious to the pens, clipboard, and assorted papers that lay behind him in a trail on the floor, dropped as he sprang across the open space moments before. When he saw Letty attempting to make her escape, he came to life.

"Wait!" He had been gnawing his lip. Now he straightened up just as though Letty were the blinding answer to some difficult problem. "You'll do. Yes, you'll do absolutely. Look, Ms. Just-passing-through, what are you doing Saturday night?"

Total incredulity halted Letty cold.

"Nothing," she blurted, out of sheer surprise.

"Terrific! I have to go to this event and you're the one I want to come with me. Kind of dance and dinner. What do you say?"

Letty felt her mouth falling open. Could this handsome, ruddy, masculine stranger actually be trying to pick her up?

The fellow paused only a fraction. Those interested eyes seemed to have taken in every morsel of her.

"Well, I see by your hand you're not married or engaged or anything. Unless you're one of those people who doesn't bother with rings. So, Saturday night . . ."

"Ah . . . I can't, I mean I don't even . . ."

Words failed Letty, causing white teeth to gleam at her. Along with the teeth, a lopsided dimple appeared, defusing the severity of his face. Letty cursed her own inability to come up with a clever rejoinder such as girls were supposed to have in reserve for situations like this. His outrageous invitation was the sort of thing that happened to spectacular girls such as her friends Melissa and Liz back at the office, but never to inconspicuous persons like herself.

"Don't even what?"

"Know you," Letty finished weakly, cursing her lack of wit.

"I don't know you either, so we're even."

The fellow tipped back on his heels again and cocked his head inquiringly. He was lean and solid and built for action. He would have rippling muscles lying across his chest, Letty found herself thinking. Naked to the waist, he would sing in the summer's heat.

"Well? I'll introduce myself first if you want? Then you can tell me who you are. Be a change from talking to dead plants."

Letty hastily diverted her mind from his chest. He seemed calmly to expect her to consider him and accept.

"No!" she cried out as idiotically as if he had just asked her to stand on her head.

Humor now glinted in those extraordinarily keen eyes rimmed with dark lashes. Such a dancing, confident humor that Letty's retreat was halted in spite of herself. The very inflections of his voice seemed to hint of truant adventure and heady impulse. Here was a man who would never be tamed with a wisecrack. Another sort of girl, some spontaneous, insanely reckless sort of girl, might actually have taken up his mad invitation. He exuded just that sort of mesmerizing lure.

"No," Letty cried out again in rising panic, scooping the plant to her bosom as she saw another extravagant remark already on his tongue.

"Hey wait!"

It was too late. The man was not used to dealing with shrinking violets. Before he could even get to the corridor, Letty vanished round the corner and was gone.

Letty zigzagged swiftly to the park and took refuge behind a large hydrangea bush while she waited for her pulse to slow down. All the guy had done was save her neck from a fall and ask her out to dinner, and she'd bolted. Brilliant! When was she going to acquire some cool?

Sighing, Letty regarded the shrunken spider plant now luxuriously awash in water from the drinking fountain. To be asked out on impulse, especially by a rugged hunk in a hard hat, was wildly unusual for Letty. Men were not her forte. Either they just didn't see her, or else they got all polite and shifted in their shoes until the moment they could escape to flashing, merry, always-at-ease-girls like Melissa and Liz. Girls who didn't freeze into tongue-tied posts when a fellow tried to flirt or tease.

"Now dear, don't you worry about men," Letty's mother had informed her after Stan Mullen had brought her home early on her sixteenth birthday date. "Someday some fellow will come along and sweep you right off your feet. That's what your father did. He laid siege. Why, I hardly knew what hit me until after the wedding ring was popped on my hand."

Ellen Smith put forth this well-worn gem with all the assurance of a woman housebound with arthritis who watched old movies every day of the week. Letty had surreptitiously examined photos of her father, whom she only remembered as a thin, scholarly looking man employed by the Post Office. His preoccupation had been raising prize hollyhocks, and he had died when Letty was nine. Letty had tried hard to imagine him young and romantic and sweeping anyone off their feet, but the effort defeated her imagination. Nevertheless, it must once have been so. Now and then Letty looked speculatively at men who resembled his type. It did no good. Even thin, scholarly fellows showed little inclination to whirl her away into dizzying passion.

Letty thought of her friends back in the sprawling, humming room where she and twenty others spent their working day. The Corral, they called it, the nitty-gritty heart of Bandis Property Management. Numbers poured in, numbers poured out. The impudent spring wind and the singing leaves were a very long way below.

Liz, a computer whiz who sat next to Letty, was a di-

minutive creature composed of devastating wit, a raging
flaxen mop, and the most guileless of blue eyes. Melissa,
in maintenance data, had a smoldering Mediterranean sultriness that wrought havoc in the ranks of her hapless fol-
lowers. Carol, tall, cool, and salty tongued, completed the
trio. The three young women were Letty's closest companions at the office. All provided the flurry of groans and racy
banter about the night before that always began their day.
All could be relied upon for tales of high drama in apartment corridors or desperate struggles punctuated by the
gearshift of a Honda. Out of natural kindness they had long
ago given up asking Letty about her own escapades.

How did they do it, Letty wondered regularly, especially
when her own dates, sparse as they were, lacked even the
gumption to make a respectable lunge when they got to the
front door. Always so popular, always so dashing, perhaps
the likes of Melissa and Liz gave off chemicals that besot-
ted men's brains or invisible vibrations that agitated every
male hormone for three miles around.

Letty liked working in the Corral but, in truth, she
thought of herself as a bit of a plain brown wren surrounded
by birds of paradise. Her simple curve of hair was about
as far away from Liz's wild mop as a style could get. Like-
wise, her gestures were gentle and her clothes came only
in soft, unstartling shades, for Letty would have reacted to
a scarlet blouse or a marigold dress the same as she would
have had someone sneaked up behind her and blown a
trumpet in her ear.

It was true that Letty had never been the type to make
an impact in a room. Rather, she had a quiet, unobtrusive
way of gliding about that made people feel she had always
been there—a comfortable, necessary part of the scene.
One expected, without thinking about it, to turn and see
her neat head bent over her work or catch her fleeting,

unexpectedly warm smile as one walked by. Letty tracked rents in several of the apartment buildings Bandis managed. Whenever a snarl of receipts turned up or a heap of half legible reports, it was Letty who tackled the mess, never dreaming such jobs fell to her so often because she worked efficiently at whatever needed to be done and had never been known to complain of a single thing.

Yet anyone who looked twice would have seen that Letty's mouth was surpassingly sweet-lipped, her nose firm, and her gray eyes exactly the shade of the mists that shroud the lake on smoky autumn mornings. Soft, impenetrable mists that could make a step off the beach seem like a step off the edge of the world. In short, Letty was that most intriguing of creatures, a woman of untapped possibilities poised on the brink of life, an overlooked package in silvery paper which might, when opened, contain the most fabulous surprise of all.

Letty wasn't thinking of future possibilities but about the present unsatisfactory state of her life. Much as Letty enjoyed the morning-after tales tossed about in the Corral, it was just a bit humiliating to be almost twenty-three and have so little to contribute. Yes, Letty admitted to a sober audience of sparrows, she would have liked to have had one or two adventures—small adventures—of her own.

But you've just turned down an adventure!

Those very pale amber eyes, that intensely alert energy crackling out from the man in the annex flashed again into Letty's mind and would not be banished. Definitely not the scholarly sort. Oh wouldn't Liz and Melissa gape if they could see her with him!

Letty indulged in the reckless fantasy for five whole minutes before she came to herself again. How could she even contemplate something as mad as accepting a perfect stranger's invitation—especially one with a devilish dimple and a gaze that could make her whole midriff quiver.

Yet the restlessness implanted in her by the rollicking surges of spring made a small, perverse part of her wish she *had* taken him up. All around, romance was flourishing. It seemed to fill the air and occupy everybody's mind. Young couples were everywhere. Old couples held hands. The lilacs along the park fence had burst into dizzyingly fragrant blossom. In front of Letty even a tough, frostbitten old reprobate of a pigeon swaggered about, feathers puffed up, trying to impress a lady friend fluttering at his side.

Despite his unorthodox approach, the man in the annex looked as though he actually would have shown up Saturday night, just as promised, to take her dancing. He had fixed on her as if she really was the only woman in all Toronto he wanted to take with him. A lightning strike of a decision . . .

Oh yeah, right, cut in the prim voice at the back of Letty's mind. Let's talk about farfetched notions! And let's notice he hasn't made the slightest attempt to follow. You probably evaporated from his head the moment you trotted out of sight.

Letty sighed and looked at her watch. If only she could remove his handprints from her body as easily.

Chapter Two

Letty soon found she was wrong about the man making no attempt to track her. She was walking down the corridor only the following afternoon, a great armful of month-end reports stacked against her bosom, when who should she see striding along but Mrs. Shelbourne herself. Mrs. Shelbourne, vice president of Bandis Property Management, changed path abruptly at the sight of her employee.

"Oh, there she is," the vice president exclaimed. "Letty, just a moment."

Letty halted apprehensively. She had scarcely ever passed more than a humble nod with such high brass. What on earth could this formidable lady want with a mere member of the troops like herself? Is it the plants, she wondered, acutely aware that against the folders she clutched a jam jar full of geranium slips which she had promised to root for Ivan down in sales. Have I finally overrun company patience?

Then the tendons tightened at the back of Letty's calves and she began to look the way a deer must look caught on the track by an approaching train. Behind Mrs. Shelbourne strode the very fellow who had stopped Letty's fall in the construction area.

Magnificent in apricot linen, Mrs. Shelbourne stopped in front of Letty. The man halted a step behind her. Gone were the hard hat and work shirt. Today he was dressed in a rich, dark brown suit and a tie that had to be real silk. He also sported an expression of calm concern, calm innocence.

"We were just looking for you," Mrs. Shelbourne told Letty. "Garner here couldn't exactly locate you, so he called me. I understand you're accompanying him to the Spring Fancy Gala this Saturday. He has some information he neglected to pass on."

Under her polite demeanor, it was obvious that Mrs. Shelbourne could hardly contain her curiosity and the wild speculation going off like firecrackers inside her head. Her companion gravely ignored all this and nodded to Letty as though he had known her for the past five years.

"Hard to find anybody inside these big buildings. I wanted to say I'll be along to pick you up about seven. I had your address scrambled too, but Mrs. Shelbourne straightened me out."

His single dimple flickered with very devilment. The disturbing pale eyes in that tanned face did not waver.

"I'm so glad someone from Bandis is going to the Gala," Mrs. Shelbourne put in, still unable to remove her gaze from the employee she had scarcely noticed up until then. "With Garner's company designing the renovations on the annex . . ."

"Renovations?" Letty got out, sounding like an echo in

a jug. She was trapped behind the stack of reports and unable to move.

Mrs. Shelbourne, wonder of wonders, smiled warmly at the man by her side.

"Oh, Garner O'Neil is famous for transforming the most unlikely old buildings into new. He has so many things going we were lucky to get him for the annex. You must tell me afterward all about the gala, Letty. It's such a wonderful excuse for anybody who's anybody to get dressed to the teeth and strut their stuff."

As Letty began to recover her wits, it flew into her mind that the moment for protest was quite past. If she insisted now that she didn't even know the man, she would not only make a fool of herself, she would do much worse and make a fool of Mrs. Shelbourne.

Besides, Mrs. Shelbourne's barely concealed astonishment at the matchup sparked that wayward thing inside Letty that had first been aroused by the fragrant spring wind. *Why not?* it whispered as she thought of Liz and Melissa and Carol whose eyes would be big as teacups if they could see this scene. And if Mrs. Shelbourne endorsed the fellow, he couldn't exactly be an axe murderer.

"I . . . will, Mrs. Shelbourne," Letty murmured faintly, unable to imagine sharing personal chitchat with this imposing lady.

Behind Mrs. Shelbourne, Garner O'Neil broke into a grin. When the boss turned to leave, Garner paused a moment behind.

"You weren't so difficult to find," he chuckled in a low voice. "I just asked about where to send sick plants. My crew found four more casualties, by the way, even now being unloaded onto your desk. See you Saturday at seven!"

Much as she had longed for her own personal adventure,

Letty could not bring herself, when she returned to her desk, to tell her coworkers about the amazing Mr. O'Neil, not even when Liz asked her, in some alarm, why she looked so faint. The whole arrangement had such an unreal quality that she was certain it would evaporate if she so much as spoke a word out loud.

All the way home that evening, Letty remained in an emotional stew. First she took the subway up to St. Clair Avenue, where she lugged herself and the rescued spider plant up the escalator and onto a streetcar heading west. The masculine image of Garner O'Neil followed her like a second shadow. She was, it seemed, really going with him on Saturday to the Spring Fancy Gala.

Mr. O'Neil's methods were like nothing she had ever heard of before and they engendered a shivering undercurrent of excitement inside her. In fact, quiet Letty was more than a little shocked at the renegade side of herself that so stubbornly insisted upon seizing this mad chance. She had kept mysteriously mum all day, nursing a secret delight at how astonished her friends would be had they only known. How pleasant to be a puzzle to them after so much time being transparent as glass.

The streetcar finally disgorged Letty only a two-block walk from home. As Letty swung around the corner onto Culver Street, where she lived, her spirits automatically lifted. Such an ordinary street, Culver Street, inhabited by working folk who grumbled about the cracks in the pavement and nursed aging automobiles. The houses were mostly alike, modest and semidetached, sided with dark brick, their lawns mere strips against the sidewalk. A street at which a stranger would barely glance, thinking nothing of importance ever happened here.

Yet, to its own, Culver Street was an oasis of comfort and familiarity amidst the larger roar of the city. It even had a park shaped like a pie wedge and a bit of wild ravine in which raccoons took refuge and cub scouts could play explorer. Very little traffic that didn't belong to the neighborhood found its way through. Children could play ball in the street here, watched over indulgently by well-known neighbors. When there was sickness, trouble, or a sofa to be moved, people converged to help. Small domestic dramas were shared from house to house and there were no more interesting topics of conversation than the doings of the folk next door. Since no one seemed to move away, Letty had known everyone from childhood. She took for granted a rare urban pocket as closely knit together as any rural village a hundred years before.

Letty hurried past the Sterns' who grew tulips in military rows and existed in a state of constant warfare with squirrels, earwigs, courting tomcats, and incontinent pigeons. Next door lived Mrs. Packerson, a dear, disorganized soul who fed squirrels from her back porch, hammered bird feeders to any available surface, and kept three hairy pooches who regarded everyone's yard as their own. Across the street, in what had once been the original farmhouse on the land, four generations of Cotters jammed themselves in, including Grandpa Cotter, hardy ancient veteran of the First World War. Grandpa frequently forgot the war was over and stood on the corner shouting for the tank corps until one of the children retrieved him. Letty was at ease with the familiars on Culver Street as she was not with the outside world. It was here that she had her real life, for she was a vital cog in the Park Beautification Committee, the backbone of the annual fun fair and bazaar, a girl guide troop leader, and stalwart behind the scenes whenever the school put on a play. She fitted into Culver Street as easily as a violin fits into its case. It was simply, irrevocably, home.

As Letty turned up the walk to her own door, her nearest neighbor, Mrs. Gambo, rose up from weeding her cabbages—massive, majestic, swathed in black. No cabbage dared do other than thrive, green and obedient, under Mrs. Gambo's beady eye.

"Your mama, she sat on the porch today without her sweater. You put it where she can reach it, eh!"

"Yes, Mrs. Gambo. I'll see to it."

"That bottom step is loose, too. I send my Ricky over to fix it when he come for dinner on Saturday."

"Oh, there's a hammer in the basement. I can put a . . ."

"Ricky, he come!" declared Mrs. Gambo with finality.

Letty, from long experience, lapsed into meek silence. Though Mrs. Gambo had immigrated from Portugal the day after her wedding, the years had not wiped out her heavy accent or her wardrobe of black. They had only increased her habit of command. She was now matriarch of a sprawling clan consisting of children, grandchildren, cousins, nephews, nieces, and innumerable in-laws, her husband, Joe, being merely another of her loyal subjects. Along with his brother-in-law and his daughter, Joe ran the corner fruit store and did Gina Gambo's bidding the same as everyone else within her sphere of influence.

Against such a force, Letty had little recourse, for Mrs. Gambo included the Smith house in her far-ranging territory. She told Letty when to get a new garbage can, harried the roofer, and marched in, without knocking, to see that Letty's mother was all right during the day. If Letty so much as coughed, Mrs. Gambo appeared with some potent old country brew and stayed to see it swallowed. Such mild, pliable folk as the Smiths were putty in Gina Gambo's powerful hands.

"Hello dear," called Letty's mother from the kitchen. "I made raisin biscuits for you tonight."

Letty hung up her jacket on the hook by the door and eased down the narrow hall to where her mother stood by the stove.

"You shouldn't make biscuits," Letty scolded lovingly as she kissed her mother on the cheek. "You know mixing dough causes trouble with your wrists."

"I felt like making them today and I've managed it quite well, don't you think?"

Mrs. Smith looked proudly at the biscuits cooling in their pan as though she'd just achieved the equivalent of climbing halfway up the Matterhorn. And, in a way, she had, for Mrs. Smith suffered from a form of arthritis that made her movements slow, her walking uncertain, and, on bad days, a retreat to her wheelchair necessary. Ever since Letty could remember, her mother had been fragile and virtually housebound. Letty did everything she could to make her mother comfortable. So did the street, from the firm-handed tactics of Mrs. Gambo to the Cotter grandchildren who, for a quarter and a fistful of jelly beans, would happily struggle back with twenty pounds of groceries from the store. Isolation from the greater hurly-burly of the world had turned Ellen Smith into a sweet, unworldly woman who knitted afghans for local bazaars and depended upon Letty for any contact with the outside beyond the street. In Mrs. Gambo's eyes, she needed looking after quite as much as Letty.

"You look flushed yourself, dear," commented Ellen, sparing a resigned glance for the spider plant left by the door. "Did you have a difficult day?"

"Oh," cried Letty, falling again into a dither even as she helped herself to the biggest of the biscuits, "that's what I wanted to tell you about. I seem to have a date."

Chapter Three

All the way home, Letty had wrestled with how she was going to explain her adventure to Culver Street. She settled on painting it as a sort of social duty connected to her job. After all, it had been Mrs. Shelbourne who had set it up and this Garner O'Neil was connected to the annex renovations. However, she perhaps overdid this aspect of it when she explained it to her mother, for Ellen pursed her lips thoughtfully.

"How lovely that you're going to a gala, dear. Too bad they couldn't have just given you two tickets. Then you could have asked someone on your own."

Ellen Smith had a mild, absent way of speaking that belied her intense interest in her daughter's affairs. She had Letty's hair and Letty's features, softened and blurred by time. Enforced inactivity had increased the dreaming quality that Letty only showed in repose. It was the years of caring for her mother that had kept Letty in the small circle of Culver Street instead of the wider activities common to other girls her age. The task was a loving task and, in all that time, it had never occurred to Letty to seek a larger field.

"Oh no, I mean—"

Letty broke off hastily. The only possibility she could have come up with on her own was Mrs. Packerson's sweaty palmed nephew, Melvin. And he'd have had to be forced at gunpoint if he thought the event might part him from his T-shirt and artfully shredded jeans. Ellen left off laying out the napkins for supper. Her eyes sharpened.

"And this Garner O'Neil, you've met him, I take it. What sort of fellow is he like?"

Letty, to her own mortified astonishment, found her tongue tied and a hot pink blush galloping up her cheeks. Ellen forgot about the napkins altogether and let out a breath.

"I see," she ruminated softly, almost to herself. A tiny smile danced for an instant around the corners of her mouth before it was suppressed. "What are you planning to wear?"

"I hadn't thought of that," Letty replied truthfully, finding a new source of alarm. "It sounds very fancy. There's that fuchsia dress I wore when I was a bridesmaid at Angela Gambo's wedding. . . ."

"Absolutely not! That fuchsia color swallowed you whole."

Letty thought about Melissa or Liz, who could have knocked 'em dead wearing an old tea towel and a squint. She herself would need considerably more help.

"There's my holiday money. I could go into one of those posh shops on Bloor Street. Sequins," Letty grinned crookedly to hide her jangle of nerves, "or at least a feather boa." She grew faint around the knees at the thought of facing one of those traps for the blindly extravagant where dresses for galas were sold.

Ellen lit up delightedly.

"Then you'll look just as fancy as the rest of them, dear. What fun for you to go out and spend all that money. I hate to say it, but you are a bit of a skinflint with yourself. Every girl ought to have a wild fling once in a while."

Letty regarded her mother, wide-eyed. Never once had she suspected such frivolous sentiments from that sedate lady.

"Mom!"

"Well, I mean it. How often is a chance like this going to fall into your lap?"

"The event is for charity," Letty returned severely. "How can people get dressed to the teeth just to give money away to those less fortunate than themselves? Maybe Mrs. Gambo's crew has something I can borrow."

"Not even a new dress for yourself? I do believe I've raised a puritan!"

"Well, I'm going to donate the price of a new dress to the charity. Since I'm going to their gala, it's the only ethical thing to do, don't you think?"

Ellen raised a storm of protest but it did her no good. Despite her unassuming exterior, Letty could dig in her heels with the best of them. And the reason she was so adamant this time, though wild horses couldn't have made her say so, was the angular form of her mother's wheelchair visible in the shadows, awaiting those days when it had to be used. How could Letty frivolously buy a dress when the money might go toward getting someone out of a wheelchair for the rest of their lives?

When Letty rose to tackle the Gambos, Ellen stopped her, that odd little smile playing about her mouth again.

"You don't have to go over there. I know where there's just the thing."

"Where?"

"Upstairs. That old green trunk on the landing. In the very bottom. Bring me the box there."

The trunk, crammed with oddments, had been rarely opened in Letty's lifetime. The long, flat cardboard box, when laid upon the kitchen table before Ellen, yielded the sweet scent of roses and a drift of yellow voile. Ellen's hands strayed over it nostalgically. Her face softened with memories of another time.

"I wore it that night at the River Club when your father proposed. They had the tiniest gazebo in the garden with wisteria climbing all over it. We were caught there in a downpour and your father, well, he put his arms around me to keep off the rain and didn't stop until . . ."

Finding Letty regarding her with astonished eyes, Ellen stopped herself and cleared her throat.

"Anyway, it's a shame to waste a dress that's been lying there all these years and worn only once. I think," Ellen decided, that mysterious smile touching her lips again, "it's time it was worn again—by someone who can perhaps get the same use out of it I did."

The dress, laid lovingly in folds of tissue paper and nestled with rose-petal sachets, proved to be in pristine condition, just as Ellen had promised. It was a wonderfully '50s-style specimen with sprigged primrose folds, cinched waist, and scalloped cream neckline and cuffs. When Letty tried it on, it needed only to be lengthened at the hem. Its snug fit was a poignant comment on the willowy long-ago figure of Ellen Smith, so different from her arthritis-altered shape of the present.

" 'Yellow, yellow, catch a fellow!' You should have heard Marion Cotter chant when I tried that dress on. Of course she was only nine at the time and thought being kissed by a boy the most revolting activity she could imagine. I'll fix the hem while you're at work. You just see if it doesn't fit you like a glove by tomorrow night.''

"Are you sure you can stitch it?''

"I'm having a good week. The sewing machine and I will get along just fine.'' Curiously, the arthritis affected Ellen's hands only in fits and starts and she occupied many a day with knitting, sewing, and even crochet. "I'll call Marybelle's too and make an appointment. She'll do your hair up real nice, just like she did when you were a bridesmaid.''

Marybelle ran the neighborhood beauty parlor and did everyone's hair from nine to ninety. It never would have occurred to Letty to go anywhere else. And Letty was frankly relieved to have the dress problem solved. She could never face an excruciating odyssey through stores she had never frequented, into the clutches of intimidating saleswomen to whom she would knuckle under at the first frown. Before she could have second thoughts, she wrote up a check to the charity for a hefty chunk of her holiday savings, and plunked it the mailbox.

"So there!'' she breathed to the face of Garner O'Neil, which had been branded upon her imagination since she had fallen backward into his arms.

Despite her modest preparations, Saturday sped toward Letty like a highballing freight train. Before she knew it, she found herself enthroned in one of Marybelle's three chairs. Marybelle sculpted Letty's hair into the armor plate of curls that was her standard for any special occasion.

"Terrific hair you got, Letty. Looks a treat all curled up for a change.''

Marybelle kept Letty's hair trimmed in its usual simple curve. She thought Letty had such good hair—too light to be brown, too dark to be blond, too full of warm chestnut highlights to be ash. Long ago she had given up talking about gel and permanents and "a nice bit of streaking" in Letty's presence.

"Just so long as it holds together through the evening. That's all I ask."

"Big date then?"

Marybelle's teasing wink in the mirror clearly said it was about time Letty had a big date and she oughtn't look so anxious about it.

With a sigh, Letty explained the occasion which was, by now, discussed with lively speculation at supper tables up and down Culver Street. Mrs. Gambo had swung into action as ponderously as a she-elephant scenting danger to the herd.

"Who is this man you go with?"

"Well, I don't really know him, but . . ."

"You don't know!"

Mrs. Gambo's eyes had widened and her black bosom had swelled. She had vetted Letty's dates since the grade eight graduation picnic. They had all been someone she either knew personally or could verify through her vast network of relatives and contacts. The idea of some complete stranger whisking Letty away was shocking and unheard-of.

"I've really just met the gentleman. . . ."

"How you meet him?"

"Ah . . . in the building where I work when I was going through the abandoned offices," Letty foolishly let out. "But he really is associated with my company and Mrs. Shelbourne . . ."

"You were wandering in this empty place all by yourself?"

Letty had to nod. At this final, damning bit of evidence, Mrs. Gambo slapped scandalized hands on her hips.

"You don't go nowhere with any man you meet by yourself in a corridor. I'll get my Carlo to go with you. . . ."

"Oh no!" Letty cried in horror. "I mean, thanks, Mrs. Gambo, but it's all right. Really! I'm . . . uh, sort of representing Bandis Property Management at the event. Companies do this all the time."

Letty had no idea what companies did all the time but she had to stop Mrs. Gambo. She had an awful vision of Carlo and Garner O'Neil struggling on her doorstep for the privilege of loading her into a waiting vehicle. Carlo worked at an industrial bakery and was engaged to the fiery Lucia Fremonte. If Lucia took a dim view of the neighborly exercise, none of the three of them would likely survive.

Letty diverted Mrs. Gambo only by describing the dinner as very much akin to working overtime and strongly emphasizing that it had been approved by Mrs. Shelbourne, the boss lady. The idea of a boss lady mollified Mrs. Gambo somewhat. She identified boss ladies with herself.

"Huh, maybe. But my Carlo, he be here in half an hour if I want."

A narrow escape, breathed Letty, as Mrs. Gambo stumped home. An escape by no means certain until Letty and the forceful Mr. O'Neil were speeding on their way. Besides her black dresses and her accent, Mrs. Gambo had brought with her from Portugal positively medieval ideas of youthful propriety. Courtship among the young Gambos had to be conducted on a hit-and-run basis, the only way to dodge the matriarch's powerfully managing hand.

Though she had kept an absolute straight face in front of Mrs. Gambo, strangers made Letty nervous. What a comfort even sweaty-palmed Melvin would have been beside the unnerving prospect of dealing with Garner O'Neil.

The appointed hour crept inexorably closer. Letty retreated to her room to accomplish the difficult feat of slipping on the dress without disarranging Marybelle's closely packed curls. Something about the dress, however, suddenly made the curls look stiff and unbearably prim. Letty shook her head. Not a hair quivered. Marybelle's formal hairdos were not only sculptural, they were designed to stand up against hurricanes. Letty had worn them to special events ever since she was twelve.

Now, the restless renegade inside her grew dissatisfied. Somehow she knew stiff curls wouldn't please Garner O'Neil. Indeed, that quirk lurking at the corner of his mouth, that oh-so-tantalizing touch of pure devilment hinted he might rather be partial to fiery tresses tumbling loose over a naked shoulder in the night. . . .

"Oh stop it," Letty chided herself, shaken by the vividness of the flash. "Next thing you'll be talking to walls!"

Nevertheless, she swiftly pulled out the hairpins, brushed out the long, hard sausages, and twisted her hair into a simple knot high up on her head. A miniature yellow rosebush bloomed in a pot on the windowsill. Letty relieved it of its buds, which she tucked around the knot. Spring itself could not have added a more entrancing garland.

"Yellow, yellow, catch a fellow!" Letty grinned at herself, imitating her mother—then reverted to sobriety at the thought of the coming ordeal. Melissa and Liz would have a flock of men at their heels within the first ten minutes at a gala. Letty would be looking about for the first convenient pillar to slide behind. Her confidence faded at the prospect of trying to make small talk for a whole evening with such a man as Garner O'Neil. He would regret his impulse, she was afraid, after half an hour with her.

Oh well, Letty brightened, there was always the ladies' room, that haven for the unpursued. Without the ladies' room, half the girls Letty knew would never have survived all those excruciating, obligatory social events in the high school gym.

Because Ellen had such difficulty negotiating steps, she lived entirely downstairs, leaving the top floor of the house as Letty's exclusive domain. A domain so crammed with convalescing plants that the furniture, except for Letty's bed, was quite invisible under the mantle of greenery. The dresser vanished under a drift of hibiscus bloom. Begonias, African violets, and a speckled coleus fought for the lamp table. Ivy trailed luxuriantly down the curtains. At the end of the day, all the green gathered up the light and transformed the ordinary little bedroom into a fragrant, translucent bower in which Letty moved as gently and gracefully as though she herself were some woodland sprite gone urban and bringing her forest with her.

Tonight, Letty wished she could stay there as she swished the unfamiliar folds of the dress about her ankles. She had borrowed her mother's rather good fake pearls which now reposed upon her bosom in two gleaming strands. She barely recognized herself in the mirror, but of one thing she was certain. She was modest enough for anybody. A good thing, for Ellen's voice floated up the stairs.

"Ready yet, dear? Gina wants to see you all dressed up."

Letty drew a breath and started down. It wasn't too late to have to fend off Carlo.

"This man who come, you hear about him yet?"

Gina Gambo had had some time to ruminate and her black eyes once again snapped with suspicion. A white slaver or a convicted kidnapper was not beyond her imagination.

"Just a company associate, Mrs. Gambo. Doing his job," Letty fibbed stoutly.

"Humph!"

"Mother thinks it's perfectly all right," parried Letty, invoking the protection of parental authority.

Mrs. Gambo's black brows flew together.

"Your mamma, she a nice lady, nicest to be found, but what she know about men, I ask."

"Well, I married one," Ellen put in mildly.

Mrs. Gambo's silence broadcast her opinion of that picayune experience.

"Do you like the dress?" Letty asked, trying another tack to distract her neighbor.

Mrs. Gambo inspected the demure production and was forced to approve.

"You look nice," Mrs. Gambo conceded, softening only for a fraction of a second. "Pretty girl! You don't let this fellow put his hands . . ."

Crazily, treacherously, Letty choked back a spurt of laughter. Oh her nerves! Shot to pieces already and not even a stray cat had so far arrived. She scrambled to smother her mirth lest Mrs. Gambo remain planted in the front hall until the doorbell rang. Or worse still, yank open the door and grill Garner O'Neil before he could step inside.

"I wouldn't dream of it, Mrs. Gambo. Honest."

She kept her gaze guileless under Mrs. Gambo's scrutiny even though her resolve in the matter of being touched was strangely wavering. If she closed her eyes for an instant, Garner O'Neil loomed in her imagination. He had smelled of sunlight and clean cotton when she'd fallen against him and his breath had been warm along her neck. . . .

Instantly, Letty squelched the thought lest Mrs. Gambo pick up brainwaves and call Carlo. By the time Mrs. Gambo condescended to sail back to her own domain,

Letty's palms were hot and she fought a compulsive desire to pace.

"Oh do sit down, dear," said her mother pleasantly from the depths of her overstuffed chair. "If they've just let him out of the zoo, you're under no obligation to go."

Chapter Four

Letty barely had time to stare at her mother before three Cotter children tore down the street.

"Look at the funny car! Look at the funny car!" they yelled at the top of their little lungs.

Letty fought to the window through a mass of Boston fern in time to see a gleaming streak of scarlet picking its way through the parked vehicles of Saturday night social activity. A conveyance such as Culver Street had never seen in all its humble existence. A car that must surely have just driven out of a 1940s movie and ought to have had Laurence Olivier at the wheel. A long, low roadster with only two seats and a gleaming silver radiator, and a figure-head leaning into the wind.

"What is it, dear?" asked Mrs. Smith.

"Somebody really lost, I guess."

Transfixed, Letty watched the vehicle inch along until stymied by the dump truck sitting half up on the sidewalk just below her house. Ricky Gambo, one of Mrs. Gambo's numerous grandsons, parked there when he stopped by for supper. Ricky thumped out of the house, still chewing crusty bread.

"I'll move it, I'll move it, okay?"

Ricky throttled the truck almost onto the Sterns' precious lawn, then draped himself out the cab window to view the vision. Letty heard her mother shuffle up behind her.

"Gracious! What on earth is that doing here? A 1949 Morgan. And on this side of the ocean too. Imagine!"

Letty jerked her gaze from the car in surprise.

"Well your grandad loved old cars. Used to sit me on his knee and go through this big book he had. Now that car there he'd say was a corker. What's it doing here?"

A prickling started at the back of Letty's neck. The car, in all its racy splendor, had stopped exactly in front of their door.

No, it couldn't, it just couldn't be for her!

Letty hauled herself from the window, where she had been showcased like a store mannequin. By the time she was back against the living room wall, the bell was ringing forcefully.

"There's the door," Ellen pointed out.

Letty turned the knob. The door swung open as though on a vigorous breeze. The space was filled by a broad, masculine figure sporting a resplendent tux and those oh-so-familiar pale amber eyes.

"Y . . . you!" Letty gasped as though she had been expecting, perhaps, the sultan of Morocco.

Dark brows lifted merrily.

"And I haven't even spirited you to my chariot yet."

Garner O'Neil made an overwhelmingly real silhouette in the doorway. His impact was even stronger than it had been in her memory.

A long second ticked by. Garner's gaze traveled swiftly up and down Letty and stopped at her parted lips. His look of calm politeness crumbled into something much more vital. He tried speech again.

"You're ready, I see. I take it you still don't object to going to the gala with me."

"I . . . no, of course not," stammered Letty, to whom the very idea was beyond imagination. "I, oh dear . . . won't you come in?"

Letty was so flustered that she didn't realize she had to step aside until Garner made a half movement toward her. She scurried back and Garner stepped over the threshold, bringing with him a sense of crackling force and energy. The narrow hall seemed suddenly very full of man.

Retreat meant the living room. Garner followed. Letty saw him take in absolutely everything, even the curlicues on the wallpaper, at a single glance. Because the dining room had been closed off to make a bedroom for Ellen, the downstairs of the Smith house was quite cramped. The living room, where Ellen spent most of her time, was equipped with fat, overstuffed armchairs from another era, along with a well-worn couch. Crocheted antimacassars decorated their backs while, underfoot, the Oriental patterned rug showed the traffic patterns through its nap. Behind the television, a shallow artificial fireplace with painted bricks supported a curving mantel above which a gilt-framed mirror reflected Garner O'Neil's broad back. Letty had always loved the room simply because it had her mother in it. Now, for the first time in her life, she became conscious of its smallness, the fade marks on the drapes, the cluttered shelves of china figurines that were her mother's pride and joy. Garner, however, fixed on the feature that Letty took so much for granted she scarcely noticed.

"Plants! I knew it. From the outside, it looks as though a jungle is trying to get out. You certainly are mad about greenery."

His voice was deep and decisive as though used to issuing strings of orders. Under its social tone vibrated that same élan that had thrummed through it back in that deserted office of the annex. Garner's gaze flew to Letty, who stood dappled with the last gold of sunset and framed enchantingly by clouds of fern, still speechless. However a voice, followed by a pale veined hand, emerged from behind a rubber plant.

"She certainly is. All these are mercy rescues from the building where she works. House has looked this way since the day she started. I'm Letty's mother, by the way."

"Indeed!"

Garner located the source of the speech. The proffered hand vanished inside his warm grasp then was released as quickly as though it had suddenly occurred to Garner to control his enthusiasm near her frail bones. Ellen recovered her fingers and looked a little breathless.

"So you're taking Letty to this . . . event. That's very kind of you."

Ellen's words were so artless that Garner almost stepped on one of the ferns. He went very still, the black of his shoulders slashing emphatically into the dim pink roses of the wallpaper.

"Ah . . . yes, ma'am, you might say that."

One cheek dimpled in spite of itself. The amber eyes twinkled wickedly but the nuance was lost on Ellen.

"She should get out more. It's good for a young person to see about them once in a while. You'll take good care of her, I know."

This last was uttered with the serene confidence of a woman who had never known danger and wouldn't recognize it if it strolled into her living room—which it very well might have. Letty recovered enough to groan inwardly. Her mother went on.

"We were just admiring your car, Mr. O'Neil. A British Morgan, I told Letty. Marvelous! A real collector's item, that."

"You recognized it!" Garner turned to Letty, "Your mother recognized the car!"

His pleasure was so instant and so genuine he made one think Ellen had spotted a vein of big gold nuggets spilling out a hill. Something irrepressible bubbled up in the man, a verve, a headlong, damn-the-torpedoes gusto for life. Suddenly, Letty knew the car was not some affectation but an item Garner utterly enjoyed.

"I collect things too. These figurines." Ellen pointed to the shelves at her side. She would have tried chatting up Old Scratch himself had he appeared in her living room as unexpectedly as Garner O'Neil. She didn't seem to mind how much of the room he seemed to take up or the fact that he was standing on the one bare patch on the rug.

"Ah, you're a better collector than I'll ever be, Mrs. Smith. Very lovely."

Ellen bloomed under the compliment so smoothly said that Letty looked sharply to see whether it was sincere. Apparently, it was. Letty was treated to the sight of Garner's lanky form leaning over a mantel inhabited by miniature dancing ladies, the dear little figures familiar to Letty since early childhood, when they peopled her imaginary dramas and served as magical characters in the stories she made up.

"Oh they're not valuable or anything, but a good number were my grandmother's. That one with the chipped skirt came all the way from England in an old steamer trunk. Imagine!"

Wildly incongruous among the worn, well-loved furniture, Garner examined the china figure. All unbidden, Letty
felt a protectiveness welling in her breast. A force had entered her quiet home. A force that made her feel that all
the peaceful patterns she had known since birth could be,
without warning, rudely whirled away.

"I don't have anything of my grandmother's."

Garner seemed to utter this without premeditation. Ellen
watched his fingers run lightly over the tiny lady whose
dress, incidentally, was the exact shade of Letty's.

"Oh dear. And why not?" Ellen inquired.

Garner opened his mouth, then shut it brusquely.

"She wasn't given to heirlooms, I'm afraid."

Aha! A family mystery, Letty decided, a keen prick of
curiosity piercing her paralysis. Up close, she saw he had
slightly uptilted eyes that would have been roguish in any
man less formidable than this. His tan lay in sharp contrast
to the whiteness of his shirt, yet the forceful mold of his
lips seemed softer now than when he had come in. He
swung round to Letty, this time lingering on her dress, so
clearly from another era, and the circlet of rosebuds glow-
ing in her hair. Something in his gaze made her skin heat
from her knees all the way to her nape. Before she could
so much as blink, Garner made a half bow to Mrs. Smith,
as impulsive as it was natural. Then he offered Letty his
arm and sailed her out onto the porch.

Letty had been so absorbed by the man that she'd forgotten about the car—and the street full of people agog
with curiosity about who she was going out with. The residents of Culver Street, who otherwise would have viewed
the proceedings from their living room windows, had been
released by the extraordinary car from even that semblance
of restraint. Every single inhabitant was, if not hanging
over their porch rail, already clustered about the old Mor-

gan, lifting their children so they could peer into the interior, kicking the tires with inquiring toes.

Garner regarded them good-naturedly, not even seeming to mind the little chocolate fingerprints the Cotter children were putting all over the back fenders. As Letty and Garner progressed down the walk, the entire street fell silent, every face turning toward them like compass needles swinging to the pole. When I get back—if I get back—Letty thought, I'm never going to hear the end of this.

Garner stalked through it all with careless aplomb. Even Mrs. Gambo, standing squarely on her front steps, muscular arms akimbo, failed to give him check. Garner handed Letty in, and only when she was settled into the soft, beautifully worn leather seat did Letty realize she was sitting on the wrong side of the car. The steering wheel was firmly planted on the right.

Garner went round the other side and had his long form folded halfway in when an ancient, quavering voice shouted in his ear.

"God save the king!"

Grandpa Cotter stood rigidly at attention, his fingers flung to his forehead in salute, his wrinkled visage grave and stern. He was so very old his skin looked transparent, but his watery blue eyes still carried a fearful flash of bravery and his white hair caught the breeze in thin, unruly wisps. Garner, at last, looked truly startled.

"Salute back," whispered Letty hastily as Garner folded his form the rest of the way in.

To his credit, Garner lifted one hand in a flourish as the car pulled away, leaving Grandpa Cotter beaming after them. Letty felt a tick of admiration through her welter of nerves. A man who thinks on his feet, she decided, as Garner turned to her in puzzlement.

"Good salute. Grandpa Cotter thinks you're at least a field marshal—because of the car."

"I'm flattered."

"Next time he sees you he'll lecture you about being out of uniform. I mean . . ." Letty caught herself. "If he ever sees you again."

The quizzical amber gaze touched her for a moment.

"You live on a . . . rather unusual street," Garner commented as though testing unknown ground.

"Oh yes." Gratefully, Letty grabbed at the topic, forgetting her agitation in a rush of affection for her neighbors.

"Grandpa Cotter will be a hundred in a couple of years. He's a veteran of the Great War, you know—and nobody can convince him it's over. The war was the most exciting time of his life, I guess. You should see the dashing pictures of him in his uniform. Now he's reliving it, episode by episode. The Kaiser hasn't a chance of invading Culver Street."

She spoke of the battles she had heard about since childhood and fell back into the buttery softness of the seat. The Morgan leaped around a corner. Culver Street slipped away like a passing dream. Letty turned to find Garner with his head cocked, wearing the expression of a naturalist who has just stumbled upon some species hitherto unknown.

"The only woman I've ever met who knows all the campaigns of World War I."

The merest hint of white teeth glinted in the changeable light, a not totally irrational suggestion of the wild in his long cheekbones. It did no good to look out the window, for cars whizzed by within a foot or two of Letty's elbow. The interior buzzed with the scent of freshly ironed shirt and some spicy male cologne. Already, Letty had the sense of being in another country, a turbulent exciting space she had never dared before.

Garner chuckled, but indulgently. "Letty Smith," he said with soft emphasis, "you are going to be every bit as delightful as I anticipated."

To her dismay, Letty felt the telltale pink climbing up her cheeks. On top of everything else, this man was exactly the sort of person who flustered her the most—the sort who said outrageous things to which she had no answer. The Morgan stopped at a light, then leaped forward again. Low to the road, it had a strange, vibrating ride that seemed intimate with every ripple on the road. Letty clutched her evening bag, itself an antique, mind still reeling with the situation.

"So how many disappointed swains were there when the street discovered you were going out with me this Saturday night?"

"Oh none. I haven't had a date for a Saturday night since . . ."

Letty shut her mouth. Good grief, why not just confess that she lived under a mushroom and raised toads for fun and profit? Anyway, she meant that there was nobody like Garner O'Neil. This year she'd been skating twice with Herbie Allison and had gone to a Christmas party at which there had been a lot of Mrs. Gambo's younger relatives, many of whom could be described as male.

"Well, somebody's dating you now," Garner replied equitably. "How could I resist a woman who would risk life, limb, and company reprimand for a dying spider plant? You're famous, you know, all over Bandis Towers."

"I am not!" Letty returned warmly.

"Oh indeed you are. You're a major charitable operation all by yourself. Your house confirms it. One big plant hospital. We should get you a charitable organization number for tax purposes and start your own fund-raising drive."

He was teasing her again. Letty could see his eyes dancing even as part of her feared he might take action on his words. Nothing, she was beginning to suspect, could be put past this man.

"Ridiculous," she heard herself saying, quite boldly, into the air. "Like taking a complete stranger to this gala!"

Beside her Garner laughed, a sound that reminded Letty of dark, rich chocolate. He swung the car around a corner, brushing his jacket back from his cummerbund—a bold slash of violet Letty hadn't noticed before.

"We stopped being strangers quite a few minutes ago. Nothing for it ahead but to keep up the trend."

The amber eyes glanced sideways at Letty, again the look of an inquisitive timber wolf. Another time, Letty might have been thoroughly alarmed. Instead, a wild thrill chased through her and she sank back into the seat, caught in the runaway beating of her own heart.

Chapter Five

The Morgan pulled up with a flourish before Toronto's grande dame of stately hotels, an edifice of cream stone and imposing doorways gleaming with ornate polished brass. Before Letty could move, the doorman had flicked the door open and Garner appeared beside him. Through the polish of his manner suddenly shone the grin he had acquired somewhere after Letty's description of Grandpa Cotter.

"Deep breath," he ordered a split second before Letty stepped into an elegant, milling mob complete with barrage of cameras and staring faces. Garner's arm neatly prevented her flight back into the safety of the car. With consummate ease, he stood her up and whisked her through the mob of reporters, onlookers, and other arrivals. They gained the lobby and found it jammed with spectacular people cradling drinks and making the chandeliers tinkle with their chatter. Enough silk, taffeta, and diamonds to cover a football field.

41

Despite the mélée, Garner's arrival turned heads, especially those of women who did not miss the pair of broad shoulders standing out above the general crowd, and the confident set of Garner's profile. A number of people gazed at Letty so avidly she was certain they knew what color underwear she was wearing. Her spine went rigid and her feet, unhelpfully, rooted themselves to the rug. The brief lull broke into a whoosh of murmurs like a soft wind through forest leaves.

"Garner," someone cried as the curly head was recognized in the hubbub. Bluff hands thrust out for a handshake, slender white arms glittering with bracelets waved and beckoned.

Letty barely had time to goggle before Garner propelled her forward into a kaleidoscope of bouffant skirts, slinky drapes of silver-woven jersey, sequin-armored bodices, all punctuated by the black and white sobriety of men in evening dress. Garner's violet cummerbund stood out, an unexpected splash of emphasis accented all the more by his swinging ease of movement and his rugged, rough-hewn body underneath. A body no mere evening tux could tame into conformity.

"Garner, hello there. Great to see you. . . ."

"Howya doing, you rascal. How long are you staying in this neck of the woods?"

"Aren't you going to introduce me to the lady? . . ."

Garner sailed through it all like a full-rigged brigantine cleaving so much froth on the sea. To those who recognized him, he dispensed a raw charisma that continued to give the impression, as at Letty's door, of something bracing and fresh sweeping through the crowd, waking up those already dozy from drink, tingling the nerves, making the women, from youngest to oldest, regard him with open speculation in their eyes.

And when he paused to introduce Letty, although all he said was, "This is Letty Smith," the pronouncement seemed to carry the ring of trumpets and cymbals. Letty struggled to sort out the hands reaching out to her, the clouds of exotic perfume enveloping her, the fascinated gazes taking her in.

Garner, they want to see Garner, she told herself breathlessly, not wanting to understand the glamour she seemed to take on merely being at his side. She clutched this illusion until they bumped into a short, dumpy, dynamic figure done up in stiff clouds of tulle and teetering on the tallest, spikiest heels Letty had ever seen.

"Flo!" Garner cried. "Where have you been all this time?"

The figure emitted a raucous laugh and shook the trader's glitter of bangles weighing down her wrists.

"Casing the joint! What else! Biggley's slapping backs in the bar, Rowen's inhaling the good Scotch, and the inimitable Ms. Wong is perched in a wing chair processing every detail."

Flo could have been anywhere from thirty to fifty and, despite the fancy dress, looked as though she devoured strong men for breakfast every day. Her face, a curious racial mix that defied identification, had street-tough and streetwise written all over it. Battered, rough-boned, it could have held its own with a crocodile, save for the wry gleam that lit her eye whenever it fell on Garner.

Garner turned to Letty and swept a hand toward this puzzling creature. "Flo Stodd, my faithful assistant and good right hand. Tries to keep me out of deep hot water and sometimes even succeeds."

He winked at Flo in an entirely familiar and humorous manner. "Flo, Letty Smith, my companion for the evening."

He stepped back. Letty hove fully into view. Though Flo seemed capable of taking an erupting volcano in stride, she went through a version of what Letty had seen in the rest of the crowd.

"Well . . ." she exclaimed, as though words failed her. "Well!"

"Come on, Flo, you can do better than that."

Flo could. She thrust out a sudden hand and took Letty's own in a vigorous truck driver's grip.

"Pleased to meet you, Letty. Real pleased. I do believe our wayward Garner is on the right track at last."

Eyes narrowed with twinkling shrewdness, Flo turned to Garner. Something was exchanged between them. Oddly, it was Garner who flushed.

"Now then," Flo put in, "I'll just make myself scarce and check out the canapés."

As Flo bobbed away, Letty could have sworn the woman was vibrating with, could it be, suppressed mirth?

As the crowd grew denser, Letty could no longer deny that, for all Garner's magnetism, it was herself a number of people were straining to look at. When Letty spotted a woman actually hopping on tiptoe to have a peek, she panicked enough to start for the ladies' room. Ten steps on her way, she squeezed past a pillar only to find herself trapped between a niche with a vase and a palm tree in an immense marble pot. One second later, as though attached by a string, Garner slipped in beside her, filling up the tiny space with his very male presence. Letty tugged at her skirt.

"Have I got . . . er, anything on my dress? People keep looking at me."

Garner planted himself against the wall, those unsettling eyes sliding intimately over Letty.

"Of course everyone's looking at you. Don't you know? You're one of the most fascinating women here tonight."

His expression was that of a man nursing private knowledge that pleased him mightily.

"I don't think it's kind to tease me."

"I'm not teasing. Look over there."

Letty peeked at the main body of the crowd. Several guests, as though fighting a high wind, leaned sideways to see around the pillar. Letty, who had never attracted more than casual glances in her life, felt goose bumps parading down her spine.

"But why? Is it . . ." Letty's hands flew suddenly to her mouth as an awful conviction exploded inside her. "Oh, it is my dress, isn't it? I know it's my dress!"

The sea of shimmering gowns had finally registered. The capital sunk into clothes here would practically have built a wing of the hospital all by itself. She also understood that had she spent every penny of her holiday money on herself ten times over it would hardly have been enough. All around were rustling cherry taffetas, cascades of hand-sewn seed pearls, multihued watered silk—and here she was in a madeover dress of her mother's!

Oh to sink through the floor and never be seen again!

"Rats!" she groaned through her fingers. "I knew I should have bought myself something brand new!"

"You didn't?"

Garner unfolded his arms even as one of Letty's large gray eyes appeared.

"Well, no. I didn't see how I could spend money frivolously on clothes when the charity needs everything it can get. I thought about buying a dress with some of my holiday money but I mailed it to the fund-raising committee instead."

Several varieties of expression traveled across Garner's face, none of which Letty could identify. Again, he regarded her with that suddenly focused concentration she had felt in her living room. His mouth went straight, his lashes narrowed.

"You're not joking?"

Why is he looking at me like that, Letty wondered. After all, a person is either serious about helping a good cause or a person isn't.

"No. And now I'm not nearly dressed up enough . . ."

The impending rush of apology was stemmed by Garner's big hand closing over hers. The physical contact removed Letty's already shaky powers of speech and left her eye-to-eye with the ruffled front of his shirt.

"To tell you the truth, you might have spent a bundle. You looked so . . . er, plain that I thought you must have been to one of those shops. You know . . . where the salespeople talk through their adenoids and sell stuff handwoven by elves in the mountains of Tibet."

Letty caught only the word "plain." A fiery flush shot up her cheeks, throwing Garner into something like actual alarm.

"I only meant classy stuff. Simple and elegant and all that. I'm no expert," he admitted pretty cavalierly, Letty thought, for a man sporting a purple cummerbund.

Letty eyed him to see whether he was trying to cajole her. She would not be cajoled, even by the charismatic Mr. O'Neil. Garner's brows were looking particularly fearsome and he was leaning toward her again. Letty could not avoid seeing the pulse of his tanned neck where it met the dazzling white of his collar. Her own speeded up as Garner tucked her fingers closer.

"You look . . . what's that word they always use? Timeless. That's it. Timeless." Pleasure gleamed in Garner's eyes as though he had hit upon an idea that had been plucking at the back of his mind ever since he opened the door of Letty's house. "All these other people, they look as though they just stepped out of today's fashion magazine. But you look timeless.''

"I do?"

Letty regarded Garner warily. Perhaps "timeless" was just another way of saying "plain." "Chic" or "lovely" she could dispense with. Basic survival was what she required.

A twinkle appeared again, the private man showing through Garner's formal exterior.

"You do," he replied with conviction. "Like in those terrific old movies. Hepburn, Davis, Wyman. Great stuff."

Ah now, this was talk a veteran of a thousand Late Shows could understand. The hard thing in Letty's chest loosened perceptibly. Besides, she wouldn't have had the nerve to don those amazing dresses around her even had they been delivered gratis on a silver platter!

Letty's hand slid up to her knot of hair, glad once again that she had brushed out Marybelle's curls. Her fingers encountered the miniature rosebuds and she felt reassured. Diamonds and emeralds she couldn't come by, but one could always rely on Mother Nature in matters of ornament.

Yet even Letty couldn't guess how the tiny garland added to the daintiness of the pale yellow dress and picked up the scatter of blossoms worked into the transparent voile swishing over the silken underskirts. "Ethereal" was the word that came to mind as Letty glided about with an indefinable style that was far too old to be considered out of date. She was fortunate she possessed no diamonds, for a sweetness hung about her that the blaze of jewelry or any woven glitter would have rudely overpowered.

Letty dared to raise her eyes to Garner's in tentative confidence. For a moment, the merest moment, the two seemed to be utterly alone in the room, a moment that whirled Letty back to that other country, that fresh new country she had entered when she stepped into Garner's car. How crisp his hair is, thought Letty, going back to the first time she had seen him in the annex. And there's a scar in his eyebrow I never noticed before. Garner inclined his head, seemingly about to say something else, when a large man strode up and gripped him with both hands.

"Garner, you dog. Hiding behind a pillar with the ladies so early in the evening! Come on!"

And they were swept into it, the brilliant swirl of faces and voices that carried them round and round until Letty abandoned any attempt to make sense of it all and gave herself up to the sights around her.

The Spring Fancy Gala was, had Letty but known it, the premiere social event of the season. Though Culver Street and the inhabitants of the Corral might be oblivious to the doings of a social level so far above their heads, the movers and shakers in the city certainly were not.

The florists knew it in the orders for massive arrangements to spill fragrantly from the corners of the reception hall. The most frighteningly exclusive dress shops knew it in the rush to corner the most fabulous of the newest silk chiffons and the wittiest layered laces. The limousine firms knew it from the way their best vehicles were booked far in advance. The charitable foundation and its recipients knew it in the astounding gush of dollars that resulted from this spangled event. The single mode of admission was a donation so massive it could almost be measured by weight rather than amount.

Yet neither was it simply another excuse for mutual admiration among the staid and solidly entrenched. The spice, the piquancy of the event was drawn from the opportunity it gave for the half-bored old guard to mix with the shocking, challenging new which pushed itself in, often for the sheer fun of acting like catalysts to stir up a marvelous fizz.

Understated wool challis brushed against hair streaked with green and chains dangling from waists. Society matrons ogled young women in Chinese pajamas and eyes made up like those of intergalactic visitors. Politicians bumped elbows with very successful rappers. Trucking magnates talked volubly to opera divas. All of them were happy to rub shoulders with Garner O'Neil.

Garner and Letty joined the whirl of faces and voices that carried them round and round and finally set them down, far on the other side of the room, in the haven of a recessed doorway. Letty's eyes bore a peculiar glazed look that caused Garner to stop abruptly.

"What?" he inquired, taken aback by her color.

Letty made a groping motion. She had long ago forgotten about her dress.

"You do realize," she enunciated slowly, "that in the last twenty minutes I've been introduced to two rock stars, a prima ballerina and . . . the mayor."

"So?"

"I . . . the mayor! She shook hands with me. The mayor!"

Letty raised dazzled gray eyes and saw Garner looking at her the way someone looked who still doesn't get the point of a joke.

Why, he associates with such people every day, she realized, and felt dizzy, the way a bather must feel, floating along on sunlit waves, waking to find herself suddenly far far out on an unknown sea. Blood rushed away from her head. She looked around for the nearest door just as Garner's hand flew to her elbow.

"You're not ill or anything, are you?"

The heat from his hand and the incredulity of his question, steadied her. A crazy laugh almost reached her lips.

Oh, Garner O'Neil, she thought, you are a million miles from Culver Street. Are you ever!

"I'm fine," she assured him despite the shade of her cheeks. Part of her was petrified, part was agog, part was madly storing memories. Wait, she thought, oh just wait till mother hears!

"Good!" Garner squeezed her elbow reassuringly. "Because if we just step over to the bar, I think we might catch the premier. And we never did get ourselves anything to drink."

To Letty's profound relief, the premier was not to be found. Garner thrust something he said was a champagne cocktail into her hand and they plunged into the crowd. Over the hubbub, no one heard Letty's protests that she didn't drink.

Chapter Six

Flo surfaced from time to time, a gaudy cork bobbing up on a multicolored sea. Without seeming to, she kept her eye on Garner and Letty. Eventually, she executed a circle maneuver around an expensively dressed couple. The man put a hand through the press and gripped Garner's shoulder. Garner swung round.

"Sinclair!"

Garner shook hands briskly. The man, who was yielding corpulent youth to pinkly balding middle age, responded swiftly.

"Sinclair and Lucinda Rowen," Garner informed Letty. Then, to Letty's blank look, added, "Rowen Department Stores."

Instantly, Letty visualized the chain of Rowen stores stretching from coast to coast, with their old-fashioned, dignified interiors and squeaky flooring.

"How do you do," she got out. After all, she had already

met the mayor without fainting. "Mother and I always buy our pantyhose at Rowen's."

Rowen's mouth hitched slightly, making Letty realize what she had just said. Lucinda Rowen reached forward to press Letty's hand. Both she and her husband were looking at Letty with the same curiosity that had been in the eyes of the others Letty had met. Letty wavered before it, supposing them all to be wondering what Garner O'Neil was doing with her. Sinclair made a gesture that would have been a playful poke at Garner's shoulder had not Sinclair been so well bred.

"So, O'Neil, this is the mystery lady. You can't imagine how many people here were dying with speculation about her."

At Rowen's bluff humor, Garner's eyes became deliberately hooded and Letty's wider. All evening, come to think of it, Garner hadn't once explained to anyone about their chance meeting and his sudden whim to bring her here. Quite inexplicably, a small lump formed in Letty's throat at this piece of old-fashioned gallantry. Something rushed in her heart toward the tall man beside her.

"Well now you know," was all Garner returned enigmatically to Sinclair Rowen. "You can eat your dinner in peace."

Garner rocked back on his heels, at ease even though Rowen clearly belonged to the most established of the old establishment. Lucinda had one beringed hand lifted toward Letty when a big-jointed, roll-gaited man barged between her and her husband, almost sending her stumbling to the side.

"Garner," the fellow boomed. "How the hell are you! You're harder to get hold of than a greased pig on the run!"

Instead of a tux, he sported a heavily corded western jacket with prairie roses embroidered all over the pointed yoke and he pumped Garner's hand as though it were a rusty pump handle. Even Letty could see he was that most screaming of clichés, the fake cowboy trying to look as though he had recently struck oil. Only from the solid gold bronco holding up his string tie, this one might actually have pulled off the feat.

"Been busy, Ralph. You?"

Ralph Biggley ran his hand along his well-oiled hair as though pushing an imaginary Stetson back.

"Oh looking around at this and that. Bought up a string of stores on the Mexican border. Greek style, can you believe? Like you to run down and see if you can do them up Tex-Mex."

Rowen's face screwed up slightly, as from a bad smell. Biggley slapped him heartily on the back.

"Hey, I intend to get a hold of Garner before you drag him off to Edmonton to do up that mall thing of yours. You'll just have to wait till I'm done."

Rowen swelled visibly, but did not answer. A light snapped on in Letty's brain. Garner did transformation jobs all over North America. For people even bigger than Rowen's!

I will not gape, she told herself firmly. I will not let anybody see my tonsils. Nevertheless a sort of faintness passed through her as she grasped the magnitude of the transaction these men were so casually trading barbs over. At Bandis, because of her work, Letty knew what "a little string of stores" on the U.S./Mexican border would cost.

Yet why should she be surprised, she asked herself. If Garner was good, he would naturally be in demand—and by all sorts of people. Ralph Biggley, though, had the look of a cheerful predator who distracts his prey with a joke before he bites its head off. If he wanted Garner, Garner had better watch his back.

Yet, truth to tell, Garner looked in no danger from Biggley. More like the other way around as Garner lounged there, large and electric, natural challenge in his eyes. He seemed about to speak when he was surprised by a delicate voice at his shoulder.

"And I know for a fact, Mr. O'Neil, that you have had inquiries from as far away as Hong Kong. Our company, for example, which is expanding into international development, is quite impressed with your performance."

Everyone turned to a diminutive woman of Chinese extraction who had appeared from nowhere. She was looking at them with black impenetrable eyes and a dainty expression. She carried herself with a breathtaking poise that was only reinforced by an utterly stark, utterly chic, mindbogglingly expensive silk dress whose only incongruity was a tiny, florid jade dragon pinned at the throat. Letty glimpsed Flo vanishing amidst the forest of shoulders and wondered if she had rounded up this one too.

"Adele Wong," Garner said to the rest by way of introduction. He took in Ms. Wong's porcelain loveliness with a lazily slow glance. Surely, Letty thought, any healthy bachelor ought to let out at least one red-blooded howl.

"You sure speak English fine," Ralph Biggley put in.

Adele Wong turned her cool, veiled eyes toward his.

"I have worked with our office in Canada for ten years. We are always looking for profitable investment opportunities." Again she looked significantly at Garner. The tip of her tongue appeared briefly at the corner of her lovely red lips. "I understand, Mr. O'Neil, you've taken out substantial options on some California property."

Rowen and Biggley both swung toward Garner, a hungry gleam in their eye.

"Options!" exclaimed Biggley. "Damn optimistic,

O'Neil. But then, of course, you'd have to spend time in all that sunshine down there."

"Optimism," Garner commented easily, "is the source of all success. Isn't that true, Ms. Wong?"

Adele inclined her head and folded her hands with the grace of two lily buds bowing in the breeze. Letty felt that this woman knew to a thread how much her dress had cost wholesale and had knocked the price down to a couple of allowable dollars of profit before the helpless retailer watched her carry it off.

Neither Biggley nor Rowen seemed to be able to think of anything to reply as Garner's gaze slid over them, just the merest shade sardonic. He's playing with them, Letty realized, another wave of faintness attacking her knees. What was she doing standing here listening to such a conversation. She was way, way out of her depth. And people out of their depth could quickly drown!

Letty shook her head, cursing her ignorance. It was a shock to realize Garner had a whole life beyond this evening. A life in which he hadn't known she existed.

Garner said nothing emphatically. Rowen craned forward and Biggley opened his jaws again. Lucinda, from the side, stepped into the fray with a speed of a seasoned veteran, a bright social smile illuminating her face.

"Enough, you sharks! We're at a party. Forget about the business and let's talk about Letty. You certainly are new, my dear. I don't recall meeting you in the crowd."

Lucinda had not ceased eyeing Letty since the moment they had met. This, thought Letty, was very odd, especially since Lucinda herself was so much more spectacular to look at, sheathed as she was in sparkly green stockings beneath a frothing fantasy of emerald sequins and masses of floating chiffon—all held up by a single, gravity defying spaghetti strap.

Lucinda tilted her head in a practiced, gossipy manner. Immediately, Garner slung his arm over Letty's shoulders, tucking her into the circle of his protection.

"She's a hidden treasure who only comes out for the real thing—like me."

Rowen chuckled bluffly and Biggley turned his goggly eyes to Letty. Smiling politely, Adele began processing Letty, detail by detail. Lucinda touched Letty's arm indulgently.

"Garner looks civilized, but under that exterior he's the worst pirate you'll ever meet. The deals he pulls, why it would make your hair stand up on end!"

"Now now, Lucinda," Garner drawled. "I always play fair."

"Oh right! If the Russian army is guarding your flanks!" Laughing, Lucinda turned to Letty. "Now you really must tell us all about yourself, dear. Everyone is dying to know."

"Know what?" Letty asked, with such simplicity that the entire group was momentarily silenced. The shock of Garner's arm, so lightly enfolding her, was causing her pulse to forget what it was she was supposed to be doing.

"Why, know who you are and why we haven't met you before, and how you came to get hold of this elusive devil, Garner. You can't imagine the competition for . . ."

"Letty has lived a retiring life," Garner declared, cutting Lucinda off adroitly. "I consider myself fortunate indeed to be her escort here tonight."

Adele Wong's smooth, pale brow wrinkled in rare puzzlement. Biggley's hand went up for another shot at his nonexistent hat. Lucinda flung Garner a startled look but was by no means prepared to give up.

"Smith, Smith . . . are you one of the Rosedale Smiths

or the Smith and Smith Investments Smiths? There are so many Smiths it's impossible to keep them sorted out.''

"She's one of the Culver Street Smiths," Garner told her, his voice full of barely hidden mirth. ''Now if you'll excuse us, we're due for another visit to the bar.''

"You got me out of there pretty fast," Letty ventured as soon as they were out of earshot. Garner still had his arm around her and the closeness of it was playing havoc with the nerves along her spine.

"So they wouldn't eat you, my dear."

"I rather thought it was you they were trying to eat."

Garner laughed aloud, a rich, delighted crow drawn so unexpectedly from the imposing black and white rest of him that heads turned from several directions.

"Quite right! Didn't you see Flo working them over to me like a canny little sheepdog? Get them sharpening their knives on each other, that's her philosophy. Starts the competitive juices flowing."

Letty gave a shudder.

"You want to do business with people like them?"

"If there were a rule that said who you had to do business with, the country would grind to a halt in a week. Besides, I find the three of them very entertaining. New money slugging it out with old. Rowen leaping into the twenty-first century like a man holding his nose over a cesspool. Wong circling about, looking for new dainties to sink her lovely teeth into."

Letty's mouth twitched. And her spending years thinking Sinclair Rowen some remote, godlike captain of commerce.

"And Mr. Biggley?"

"Made his fortune in honey-wagons—ah, portable sanitation. He'd expire if anyone mentioned that out loud."

Their eyes met and Letty found herself actually sharing the joke with the man who could banter with Sinclair

Rowen. Garner fought to the bar and reappeared with a goblet.

"Another champagne cocktail."

Letty discovered that she had polished off the first. It had tasted sweet and hardly wicked at all.

"I really don't drink, you know."

"You don't?"

Now that Garner finally heard what she had tried to say earlier in the crowded bar, he looked quite amazed.

"Oh, I've had champagne at weddings. And Mr. Gambo next door makes wine every fall. He always gives mother and I a bottle or two—for head colds, of course."

"Then think of this as cold medicine."

It seemed fruitless to refuse the second when she had already drunk the first. Gingerly, Letty took it and sipped. It tasted even more delicious. Her nerves calmed and the details around her slowly resolved into a finer clarity. She stopped halfway through her fourth sip and gazed across the crowded room.

"What?" Garner asked.

"That woman there. Her dress. It looks like cast iron and it hardly comes to her armpits. How does she keep it on?"

"Force of will."

Incredibly, Garner winked and it was Letty's turn to laugh merrily under the shimmering lights which caught in her hair and shone from her gray eyes. This was the moment she realized she was actually having a tremendous amount of fun.

The crowd began to move into the great dining hall. Garner placed a guiding hand on Letty's back. Letty, who had just finished off the second champagne cocktail, felt unaccountably light. She straightened with an almost reckless grace. Perhaps, she thought, there might just be something in the Katharine Hepburn comparison after all—a bubbly assurance that evaporated when she realized they were being led to one of the front tables.

"What are we doing up here?" Letty whispered in alarm.

"Providing the entertainment." Garner pulled out a chair and settled Letty into it. There wasn't even a centerpiece to slide behind. The man on Letty's right nodded at her affably.

"Seating in order of pocketbook. You give big, you get planted up front."

Personally, Letty would rather have faced massed machine guns than that sea of upturned faces. Biggley, Wong, and Rowen were seated nearby and also glanced Letty's way. Letty was grateful all over again that the premier hadn't stayed. It was bad enough being the focus of a thousand eyes as she tried to put away her Chicken Kiev, though Garner ate as placidly as though he were alone on a patio. When he saw Letty's state of petrified inappetite, he motioned the waiter to pour her more wine. "Brace your nerves," he told her, and attacked his dessert with gusto.

Letty drank whatever was put in front of her. When speech time rolled around, she had almost relaxed—until the chairwoman began to introduce the people, making it charmingly obvious, without mentioning it in words, that they represented the largest donors to the cause. Letty's knees stiffened as the introductions drew closer. Garner was introduced. Then the chairwoman's voice seemed to ring in every cranny of the room.

"Ms. Letty Smith, to whom the committee wishes to express its appreciation."

Letty felt faint, not a single muscle was able to move.

"Take a bow," whispered Garner encouragingly, seeming to lend of his ample strength.

She managed to incline her head. A wave of applause started up as Letty half rose, then fell back into her chair with a plop, the dazzle of the crowd in her eyes. As soon as they were released from the table, Letty bolted out into a deserted hallway, dragging Garner with her.

"I had to get away from all the diamonds for a minute."

"They stop hurting your eyes when you wear them yourself."

Letty looked sharply at Garner and saw teasing in his eyes. All the hard edges of him had softened considerably and he no longer looked, as he had with Rowen, Biggley, and Wong, like the major predator among lesser teeth and claws.

"I'm hardly likely to get the chance—on my salary."

"But you admit the idea is fun?"

"I'm not sure I know what's fun or not," Letty returned with a sort of indignant asperity that had at last brought her tongue to life. "You'd think with all the money these people have, they could do a little less with diamonds and a little better for the charity. Imagine, mentioning me for the amount I turned over in that dress check!"

A most peculiar expression struck Garner's face, even though he managed to catch himself in the middle of it. The whisky eyes glowed for a moment, then crinkled with humor.

"You're right. Being tight with cash is a well-known way to get rich."

"Then there must be a lot of very rich people here."

"Indeed," murmured Garner blandly, easing forward to brush a tendril from Letty's forehead. "How about we mingle with some of them? I hear the band."

Chapter Seven

I *didn't know music could make you fly,* Letty thought, in a state of pinwheeling wonder. *I didn't!*

After dinner, the crowed spilled onto the dance floor. Letty found herself in Garner's arms, floating under huge chandeliers dimmed to winking gold. They moved to a waltz, a slow waltz, fortunately, since the experience of suddenly being so close to Garner did treacherous things to Letty's feet. The music seemed a protection from fascinated eyes as people grew absorbed in each other or lost in the crush. After a few moments, Letty forgot the others altogether as her fingers absorbed the texture of Garner's tuxedo and his lapels rustled so near her face.

It didn't matter that her dancing was uncertain. Garner danced with sweep and verve. Once in his embrace, Letty felt herself carried away so strongly it wouldn't have mattered whether she had feet or not. She spun and dipped, light as dandelion fluff adrift across the fields. Champagne cocktails and a good deal of dinner wine, intoxicants practically unknown to Letty's system, gave her wings of her own.

In the live orchestra, the establishment had exerted its privilege, and the cello throbbed through Letty's bones. Garner, by subtlest pressure, drew Letty closer until they were cheek to cheek. The touch of his warm skin against her own sent tremors down through her limbs. Her fingers tightened involuntarily on his shoulder. Without need to know where she was going, Letty closed her eyes and stepped into the musical dream that lifted her away from any ordinary existence she had ever known. The crowd, the room, the chandeliers, everything vanished into the humming rhythm of moving together with Garner. She drank up the revelation of it, the breathtaking new knowledge that one could exist in sensation only and in distilled delight.

Could she be imagining it, she wondered in her state of drifting haze, or was Garner nuzzling his face into her hair? He moved, oh how he moved with her in such splendid unison, as if their bodies had found some unspoken means of communication, some new language they were each just beginning to use.

Letty's bliss with Garner lasted until a large, heavily breathing body invaded their charmed space.

"Share the wealth, O'Neil. You can't keep the marvelous Letty Smith to yourself all evening."

It was Sinclair Rowen, giving off the fumes of pricey Scotch, pink pate flushed, eyes glinting with what he imagined to be rakish deviltry. Garner hesitated a long fraction, then yielded as grandly as he had swept Letty up.

"Far be it from me to deny Ms. Smith her moment when there's men lined up around the block!"

Rowen took over. The move seemed to send a signal all around the dance floor, setting off a struggle to dance with

Letty. Rowen got only about two turns before a steel mag-
nate cut in, then a city alderman, a studded-leather singer,
a decathlon athlete, and a master of the North Toronto
Hunt.

This mad, bewilderingly unreal succession of partners
quite went to Letty's head. The enjoyment with which she
had danced with Garner transformed itself into a benevolent
glow which enveloped everyone from the fire marshal to
mouth-breathing Ralph Biggley, and would have happily
extended to the Hunchback of Notre Dame had he showed
up to get his turn.

Letty felt—fascinating. Indeed, almost like the most fascinating woman at the gala, as she coped with a crush of
partners who barely had time to say their names before they
were supplanted. Incredibly, unbelievably, it must be so, or
why else would all these men be struggling for the privilege
of half a circle about the jam-packed dance floor?

Letty gave up trying to make sense of anything. The only
possible explanation was that magic actually did exist and
she, Letty Smith, had stumbled into a shower of fairy dust
and been transformed. The only given, the only fixed point
to it all was a single, shiveringly overwhelming man—Garner O'Neil.

The child in Letty, the child she never guessed existed,
the good child who had sat demure and polite at countless
gatherings, the quiet Letty so diligent in the Corral, leaped
suddenly from uncomplaining obscurity and revealed herself laughing, joyous imp filled with energy and light. Letty
felt beautiful, mesmerizing and, yes, actually devastating.
Who cared why! It was the headiest experience of her life.

Though the crowd became but a musical blur in jeweled
hues, Letty never lost her awareness of Garner. All her
senses, tuned like fine antennae, followed Garner about,
seeming to feel his every move even when she couldn't see

him. Like Letty, he danced with other partners, everyone from the ladies of the organizing committee to Adele Wong, who moved with the same logical, fluid grace with which she did everything else. Adele gazed unblinkingly at Garner, storing every detail away. Her lovely lips curved in the smallest of satisfied smiles, hording some secret anticipation known, for the moment, only to herself.

Garner grinned at Letty each time he went by just as though they had a pact, a perfectly understood conspiracy between them—Garner's gift so that Letty could have the full savor of the gala. He bent his head over his partners, chatted amiably, waltzed them in his dark-clad arms. But he never, Letty noted in satisfaction, drew any woman to dance against his cheek as he had with her.

With unquestioning joy, Letty accepted Garner's offering. Because she did so, she rode the rainbow freely, giving herself over to the enjoyment, swimming in the sensation of not being herself, not the Letty Smith who checked numbers all day and struggled home on the subway. She was now some other Letty Smith, some fabled being her everyday self would be unable even to imagine. The new Letty laughed boldly aloud and made dashing remarks to the men who struggled for her attention. The new Letty twirled and spun, flung into the unheard-of, unimagined sensation of being a positive object of competition among the men.

The men, as they danced, all tried to ask Letty about herself, in not-so-subtle ways attempting to find who she was and what she did and how she came to be with Garner—a curiosity which Letty became determined not to satisfy. Why ruin her enchanted evening by hauling out her everyday life or revealing that it was only by random chance that she was here and not at home reading novels in bed. The more interest her partners expressed, the more laughingly elusive Letty became. Scarlett O'Hara couldn't have done better. No indeed!

She knew she was tipsy for sure when she informed the police commissioner that her name was really Laetitia, "which means," she chirped, " 'Delight' in Greek!"

When Garner reclaimed her, it felt like coming home. The giddy, reckless mood had blotted out Letty's sense of time, so it came as a surprise to find they were circling a great ocean of space on the previously crowded floor. All around, people were yawning and blinking and making their way to the door.

"We're going to be dancing all by ourselves pretty soon," Garner murmured.

"It seems hardly a minute since we started."

"Does it?" Garner bent his head over her hair, now softened by drifts of straying tendrils. "It's been hours."

Letty looked even more startled. She wasn't tired at all. There were miles of waltzing left in her feet.

"But . . ."

She stopped. After all, even Cinderella had to climb back into the magic coach and go home. Halfway home, the coach had turned back into a pumpkin.

Garner searched her face, which was flushed from the dancing and infused with the radiance that comes only from nearly perfect happiness. The planes of his face changed once again.

"All right, Delight in Greek," Garner murmured, with an air of both decision and inevitability. "We'll take care of the rest of the evening by ourselves."

A thrillingly forbidden shiver slid down Letty's spine. Wordlessly, she dashed to the ladies' room, her first visit of the evening, and without a thought of hiding out. The powder room was exceedingly elegant, divided into an inner and an outer region with flatteringly lighted mirrors, gold wallpaper, and Empire lounges. A mob of spectacularly dressed women was giving their faintly disheveled selves last pats before the journey homeward. Letty, obscured by the crush, could not avoid overhearing conversation, of which she formed the principal topic.

"Who is she anyway," a woman was asking as she leaned forward to pluck at one of her eyebrows. "I asked Garner straight out and only got a grin for my trouble. I guess he intends to let us expire with curiosity."

"Clever devil," responded another indulgently. "If he wanted attention tonight, he certainly got it—all without having to do a single thing except escort this Letty and be his roguish self."

"Did you see Biggley and Rowen, practically stepping on each other's feet to get a dance!"

Someone else laughed.

"Indeed! We sure have to give Ms. Smith credit for nerve on this caper. She's the last sort you'd imagine as Garner's type. And he never took his eye off her either. Maybe old Garner is finally slowing down."

Incredulous hoots went up all round.

"That'll be the day!"

"Anyway, Ms. Smith sure must be loaded, considering what she forked over at the auction. How wily of her to do it through an agent, so no one would guess. Wish I'd thought of it myself."

"My dear, that would put a hole in even your Christmas money. I wonder if she's from one of those reclusive northern mining families. That dress was such a wonderful period piece . . ."

The voices all suddenly died as the crowd realized Letty was in their midst. The woman who had been speaking flushed, then made an agile recovery. She rustled over to Letty in a mass of tangerine silk and extended her hand.

"I'm Alicia Whiting," she said warmly. "Please excuse our bad manners but really, we're just admiring your enterprise. You can't imagine how many have tried to rope in Garner O'Neil and come up empty. Some of us even bid against you. Ran the price right out of sight, I'm afraid. Of course that only means you've been unbelievably generous to the fund-raising effort. It eased our consciences to see you having such a good time tonight."

Letty barely heard the woman. All she could think of was that these people seemed to have thought she had somehow *bought* this date with Garner. Her eyes came back in focus on the multihued crowd eagerly inspecting her.

"Ah . . . yes, a very good time."

Letty took one step back, then two, groping for the door.

"And remember," she heard Alicia Whiting call out cheerily behind her as she fled, "the night isn't over yet. Make sure you get your money's worth . . ."

"I . . . already have," Letty stammered. And fled.

Chapter Eight

Garner was waiting for Letty, ready to leave. Again, the tremor vibrated through her. The conversation in the ladies' room had flustered Letty. She suddenly realized this was no callow boy trotting at her heels but a fellow in the full, prowling prime of his manhood. He hovered above her, solid, virile . . . unnerving. What did men like this expect at the end of their dates? And how did women who danced all evening in their arms cope with them?

Swallowing very hard, Letty tried to speak. No sound came out as Garner's hand found the small of her back and guided her out to where the car was waiting, this time with the top down. The sweet night air poured over Letty's cheeks and the gilded facade of the hotel fell away as the low old car leaped forward. As they sped through street after deserted street, Letty's chest grew tighter. How intensely aware could you get, she wondered, of a man's hands on a steering wheel, the movement of his thigh as his foot touched the gas. He filled up the car's interior as light from passing street lamps alternately washed his features with palest gold and darkest shadow. The car slipped through sleeping houses and rolled to a stop not a dozen yards from Lake Ontario. Garner shot off the motor. The band in Letty's chest loosened as she recognized the place.

"Why, the Boardwalk!"

The Boardwalk was a precious, romantic stretch of shore preserved whole in a city of wharves and waterside expressways. Green park and trees buffered it tenderly even from the low wooden houses behind. Massive willows hung protecting arms over the wooden promenade, which curved away in the dimness. Pale sand ribboned into a broad border. The lake beyond shimmered with a living brilliance under a lopsided, three-quarter moon. Over it all, the promise of summer hung as palpably as a song.

"You've turned awfully quiet," Garner smiled, making himself comfortable.

Letty laced her fingers and took a breath. It was a night for reckless pronouncements. She might as well go the limit.

"The women in the ladies room . . . they all seemed to think I had bought this date with you. By auction."

For a fleeting moment, Garner looked sheepish as only a brigand could look, caught doing a good deed.

"The papers might pick it up tomorrow, so I might as well tell all. You did buy this date."

"I did?"

Such comical bewilderment flitted into Letty's eyes that Garner laughed softly.

"It was all because of Flo. She volunteered me as an auction item at this fund-raiser—the prize being a date with me at the gala. Of course Flo only got around to telling me about it at the last minute, so I had to move fast."

The luxurious old leather creaked under Garner's weight while the breeze knocked a shock of hair across his forehead. Letty's mouth popped open and remained open despite all the childhood admonitions about not making a trap to catch flies.

"It was you! You bought up that date at the auction! That's why you fixed on me so fast!

Garner threw up both hands in open capitulation. His brigand grin flashed back.

"Guilty as charged."

Perhaps he didn't expect Letty to be so dumbfounded.

"I had to do it through a third party, of course." His eyes twinkled. "The agent got a run for the money. I had no idea I was so valuable."

"How . . . much did the agent have to pay?" Letty asked, even as she wondered how her own voice could quaver like that. Garner lifted one shoulder negligently.

"Enough to make the charity very, very happy."

A multitude of expressions galloped across Letty's face.

"I can't take credit for a . . . a donation of that size!" she cried in a panic.

"Afraid you'll have to. Unless you have a heart of stone, of course." Garner turned those amber eyes full on her and gave a look that would melt granite. "A fellow can't let it get out that he bought a date with himself, can he? And paid a fortune for it too."

"But I can't . . . lie!"

Letty's earnest, genuine shock caused Garner to pause. A nightbird flitted up into the sky and silence made a perceptible beat between the couple in the car.

"I daresay you can't," Garner replied, oddly grave. "And that makes it worth every penny it cost."

Letty felt a hitch inside. The night silence intervened again as she looked up with a questioning gaze. She thought she caught a wicked sparkle in Garner's eye, provoking an answering bubble inside her. Some welter of nerves produced a tinkling laugh.

"All right, no . . . no comment," she gasped out.

When her mirth died, Letty found herself facing Garner under the sighing willow trees. Words seemed to have fled. A feverish flame ebbed and flowed around the one question swelling within her, the one she could no longer repress. All her deep, sweet intensity glowed from her eyes.

"Why?" she breathed. And they both knew what she was asking.

From the sudden agitation around Garner's mouth and the way he began to tug at his collar, Letty guessed that he was used to banter and laughter with women, not such directness. Was he a man who dealt only in bright surfaces, she wondered uneasily. But she could not withdraw her question.

For a long moment, Garner regarded the luminous simplicity shining around Letty like cloak. Then his customary smile fought back. An adventurer plunging his hand into a treasure horde, he reached boldly for an answer.

"Because that's how I work—from the very first venture I ever put together. I believe in quick decisions. People think I'm a clever entrepreneur, but you know what it really is? A hunch, a conviction in my gut, a crazy little voice at the back of my head telling me this is the way to go. That little voice was shouting its head off when you came tumbling down clutching that dead plant to your bosom."

Letty first felt her earlobes turn pink.

"And that's why everyone was so . . . interested in me, wasn't it? Because of the auction."

Letty thought of all the times she had ornamented the wallpaper or had her feet stepped on by reluctant partners.

The bubble around her might have burst had not Garner turned toward her.

"Partly. But men wouldn't have fought to dance with you if you hadn't been a genuine human magnet. Who was I to frustrate all the fellows feeling the pull?"

Yes, Letty believed him. She had been a magnet. For the first time, she had tasted the true power of the feminine and it proved an almost overwhelming draught.

The sighing of the willows seemed to die as Garner turned. Slowly, he stretched out his hand and traced her chin, his touch running lightly, like the cool-hot tingle of snow, over her skin.

"Did it ever occur to you," he rumbled slowly, the merest note of weariness brushing his voice, "how many men out there are starved in their hearts for a fresh spring breeze?"

Letty felt a lurch in her midriff and stared up questioningly—for the man actually looked serious. When his finger reached the very tip of her chin, just beneath her lower lip, it lingered there, then fell away abruptly as Garner caught the look in Letty's eyes. He retreated behind a teasing grin.

"Shall I go on? Shall I talk about a single sunny wildflower outshining a roomful of hothouse blooms? The invitation, the novelty . . ."

Letty emitted a small breathless sound. A warmth started at her toes. She knew men of the world were supposed to say extravagant things, of course, but this outdid even her expectations.

And she might as well enjoy it while she could!

She thought his dimple flickered roguishly and the maverick in her, the new, daring Letty, responded with a laugh low in her throat. Garner tugged his bow tie loose and stuffed it in his pocket. Without it, his shirt loosened, revealing a tantalizing triangle of tanned masculine flesh. When he turned his head, his face fell into shade.

"You think I'm joking, don't you?" he murmured, resting a lean hand back on the steering wheel.

Now the warmth had reached Letty's head, as though she were a bottle being filled with some rare, intoxicating liquor. She caught the sharp spice of his aftershave and there was a certain smokiness about his voice. She was overcome by a momentary sense that she was really perched atop a very high pinnacle—and about to step out into space.

The sensation came and went in a flash, and when it was gone, Letty struggled for more familiar ground.

"I've cost you a fortune," she protested. "Surely there are lots of women you could have gone with for free."

"Indeed there are. But not a single one of them is Letty Smith. Now let's have a look at that shore."

Before they could get into the matter further, Garner opened the door and ushered Letty out onto the Boardwalk. He took off his jacket and slung it over his shoulder.

"I'm glad we're on the Boardwalk," Letty told him. "I used to come here all the time as a child. Mrs. Gambo used to take the whole tribe from Culver Street swimming. She'd plant herself in the sand like the Rock of Gibraltar and none of us would dare get out of our depth and drown!"

"Didn't your parents bring you?"

"Oh, sometimes, if somebody had a car and would drive. You see, mom's always had arthritis and it's tough for her to get around. Dad hated to leave his gardening to broil himself in the sun. It didn't matter. There was always somebody from the street going to the beach."

Letty began to smile. The Boardwalk was one of her favorite spots in all the city. Warmed by memories, she beamed up at Garner as though this stop was a special treat

Garner alone could have come up with. She thought of the other gifts of the evening.

"Thanks. For letting me have all those dances back there. And . . . everything."

"Everything" included the privilege of going, Garner's protectiveness in that inquisitive crowd, and simply the way he had looked so heart-stoppingly handsome under the cut-glass chandeliers. "You must have quite the reputation if so many ladies ran the bidding up on you."

Now why did I say that, Letty groaned, taken aback by both her own audacity and the suddenly changed, charged atmosphere her words seemed to produce. Garner's profile cut sharply into the yellow light falling from the lamp behind them. What if he actually did live up to such a reputation!

A wild beating set up inside Letty, and she flew into a flurry to divert him. Frantically, she cast about for something neutral to say.

"Where did you swim—as a boy, that is?" was all she could come up with. It worked, though. Garner had to do a quick shift to follow Letty's erratic turn of thought. He also, as in Letty's living room, seemed deliberately vague.

"Here, there, and everywhere," he murmured as a flock of sleeping gulls floated like lilies scattered under the moon. The tangy scent of the lake and the quiver of the willow leaves immediately surrounded them. They strolled slowly along the gently curving promenade, the wooden planks echoing dimly under their heels. Letty felt her breath smooth happily and the breeze caress her face. The misgiving that had gripped her when they set out in the car had vanished. She felt safe with Garner now.

Well . . . almost safe. She couldn't still the erratic pace of her heart—or avoid the knowledge that it was unbearably exciting to be walking along in the dappled darkness with such a man on such a night, with the moonlight streaming down and his arm brushing hers. She couldn't forget his touch on her skin. It would only take the smallest movement for him to . . .

Swallowing hard, Letty pushed the idea away. Or tried to push it. After all, it had to be the first thing a girl would think about at the end of such an evening. What was Garner thinking, she wondered. Or planning?

Letty stole a glance at him and received again almost a physical shock at the bigness of him and the way the blackness of his attire made him so vivid under the willows. Something in her abdomen tightened thrillingly. Not even Melissa or Liz could have experienced such a man as this!

"So tell me about Letty Smith," Garner said at last, lightly, softly. "Who is this lady who lives in a little house packed with plants and dances divinely at balls?"

He was smiling down, looking mellow. Under the quizzical, teasing quality vibrated a genuine desire to know. Absorbed in his closeness, Letty took a moment to grasp the question, then flung back her head.

"Oh, there's nothing to tell. I work at the office and come home every night. My father's dead and I live with my mother. Quite contentedly, I might add."

"That's it?"

"Of course."

A short, irreverent laugh shook the night air.

"The heck it is!"

Letty turned such startled eyes that Garner had to grin.

"What I mean is, still waters run deep."

"Oh that!" Letty was tickled at being the subject of a cliché and a proverb at the same time. "Still waters might run deep, but they might be just as still at the bottom as at the top. Have you considered that?" she chuckled, feeling excessively bold.

"No. And I don't believe a word."

Even in the gloom, Letty sensed his gaze catch her. Again, as at her door and a number of times through the evening, Letty could feel Garner looking at her—really looking at her. His very intentness made her feel laden with untold possibilities and depths unplumbed. Perhaps, she thought, with an awesome leap, she really was a woman of mystery to Garner. The very idea made her feet want to skip and she fought a desire to shake her hair loose in the breeze. She laughed aloud, released from her last constraints by an unheard-of, improbable, utterly enchanting notion.

"Bet you can't climb those monkey bars," she flung out in the sort of completely illogical non sequitur people resort to when they simply must express the exuberance inside.

She got him there. He stopped stock still and looked perfectly flabbergasted.

"Well," Letty went on, defending her mad suggestion, "I have my opinion about you too. And I think . . . I think you're far too dignified. At least for out on the Boardwalk."

Amazing! She, who couldn't hardly think of a thing to say to pale, unthreatening Eddie Horner, was making unheard-of remarks to the formidable Garner O'Neil. Hurrah for champagne cocktails!

Chapter Nine

The Boardwalk was bordered by a second trail, asphalt, for all the runners, cyclists, and fitness fanatics who poured through the neighborhood. Alongside the trail, the city had installed assorted exercise paraphernalia for those who wanted to further torture themselves. Beside Letty stood a set of monkey bars on three levels to suit all sizes of human beings.

For a moment, Letty thought she'd gone too far. Then Garner dropped his jacket to the grass.

"Bet what?" he demanded, leaping up so that he hung by his hands from the highest bars.

A kiss, cried Letty's heart and she barely prevented herself from singing it aloud. She wondered if her lips had moved, for Garner suddenly grinned like a scamp and propelled himself hand over hand the entire length of the bars. He seemed overtaken by an attack of animal high spirits.

"For you," he averred in a voice that was both pointed,

meaningful, and merrily intimate, "I'll do even better! Want to see me walk the top?"

"Oh no!" croaked Letty, suspended between horror and delight. The top seemed impossibly high and skeletal. "You'll fall off."

Letty could only throw up her hands, buoyed by the incredible knowledge that, on top of the train of events that had rocked her tonight, Garner O'Neil was trying to impress her.

"Wait . . ."

With a compact, powerful thrust of his body, Garner swung his legs up to the top of the bars, levered the rest of himself up, and scrambled erect, teetering far, far above the ground.

"Okay, okay, you win! Come down," Letty called out, feeling suddenly that if he fell, the world would be blotted out.

"I never back down on a challenge."

Without his jacket, the wide cummerbund looked like a swashbuckler's sash embracing the whiteness of Garner's shirt, which already had ruffles and needed only great flowing sleeves and a couple of sword slashes to suit Errol Flynn on the deck of a privateer. Here was the man who had toyed with Biggley, Rowen, and Wong. Instantly, Letty divined the secret of his success—a raking reach for whatever he wanted, fueled by a fierce, damn-the-torpedoes thrust through life.

Alive with springing muscle, Garner padded easily as an alley cat along a beam not even as wide as his foot. Then he turned, padded back, and stood above Letty, his arms spread wide in triumph. With a knifelike unfolding of his body, he dropped onto the sandy earth at Letty's side, favoring her with his timber wolf grin.

"You seem pretty fond of risks," Letty said weakly,

gulping with relief at Garner's safe landing—and the awareness that she had stirred him into an aliveness she hoped she could handle.

Garner retrieved his jacket and slung it over his shoulder.

"Not risks. Challenges. Things that depend on your own raw nerve and nothing to do with luck."

For some reason, his mood had taken another quicksilver turn. As they set out again, his jaw looked hard.

"Have you got something against luck?" Letty tossed out, wanting them to get back to where they had been before.

Garner only grunted. Letty hurried a couple of steps to keep up with him.

"No, tell me!" Incredibly, she was holding on to his arm, determined that he should not break their glorious mood.

Garner grunted again, this time at Letty's touch. She did not fail to note the muscles, still warm and flexing from their workout, underneath the fine fabric of Garner's sleeve.

"Luck is for fools!"

Or for people blind chance happens to match, Letty thought happily. Lost in the feel of rampant masculinity under her fingertips, she wasn't even aware of how her grip tightened.

"Sounds like you've had encounters with a few such fools."

Garner stopped dead on the Boardwalk and looked down full at Letty, one brow shooting upward.

"Oh, I didn't mean to pry," Letty put in hastily.

They started walking again. And then, suddenly, into thick silence surrounding them, Garner said, "My father was a gambler: ponies, pools, lotteries, anything going. A man with the golden touch—in one hand, that is. The other could lose him the pot in a wink."

Beyond perhaps a two-dollar racetrack bet, Letty had never believed actual, real-life gamblers existed.

"His whole salary?" she asked incredulously. "From his job?"

Garner's lip curled.

"Job! Pop didn't have a job. He would have considered it an indignity. Feast or famine, that's the way it always was with us. Once, we were so far behind in our rent we had to sneak out the back window of our flat and leave our furniture behind."

Letty had read about such stuff, but never supposed it actually happened.

"Wasn't your mother . . . well, angry?" she ventured, thinking what would happen should say, Vern Cotter or Joe Gambo pull such a stunt. The funerals would be the very next day.

Garner stopped again. One corner of his mouth lifted into an odd smile, half open, half closed. He drew his fingers through his hair.

"You make a fellow talk too much, Ms. Smith. It's a dangerous thing, having you close by."

Letty blushed hotly even as her pulse jumped with pleasure at his words. She supposed a date sold by auction would naturally be shameless with compliments and brimming with easy charm.

I don't care! cried the newly formed renegade within. She couldn't help thinking his shirt fit him like a pelt fits a wolf. The lake existed as a background for him, the band of moonlight lived to silhouette his lithe dark figure against the shining water.

They strolled on until a cool gust stirred the leaves. Garner slipped his jacket over Letty's shoulders, tugging it smooth at her throat, the move as simple and intimate as an embrace. His warmth still clung in the folds. Letty quiv-

ered involuntarily under the unexpected solidity of the gar-
ment, the sense of Garner, his shape, his spicy masculine
scent inhabiting the folds. Sliding his arm easily around her
waist, Garner drew her along the Boardwalk, which Letty
saw was not deserted after all. Seated in the shadows,
perched on the tumbled stone breakwaters, strolling with
dreamlike slowness over the grass, pairs of lovers fitted
everywhere into the landscape as if nature had grown them
there.

Lovers! The word swept through Letty like a perfumed
wind from a continent she had never known existed before.
Letty, who had just drunk champagne cocktails for the first
time, whose life was as ordered as petit point embroidery,
found herself stirred deep in her abdomen at Garner's spoor
of forbidden wildness.

"Now that we're exchanging family secrets," Garner
murmured in a low, thoughtful voice, "why don't you tell
me more about Culver Street?"

Why the topic fascinated him, Letty couldn't guess. Yet
she took refuge from the agitation of her own pulse in the
familiar details of her everyday life, details she wished to
share with Garner as much as she had wished to shield
them at the dance. They walked more and more slowly,
while Letty talked. And talk she did, her tongue loosened
as never before with any stranger. All unknowingly, her
face gentled and smiled with loving kindness in the moonlight as she painted the simple rhythms of her life, the care
she took of her mother, her place in the interconnecting
web of people on the street. She spoke of her friends at
work, even her endless exasperating family of orphaned
plants, revealing, without knowing it, her goodness of heart,
her quietly shining soul.

Their steps echoed quietly while the Boardwalk lights,
dim as Chinese lanterns, shone in a yellow nimbus among

the willow leaves. As they moved, Letty found herself speaking more and more slowly until finally, words deserted her. What need was there of words when moonlight sparkled so brightly on the sand, when edges of white foam murmured to the shore, when honeyed languor stole so subtly along her limbs?

The very silence around Letty and Garner became passionately friendly, two strange nations meeting and knowing instantly they must be allies. Again, Letty had the sensation of having wandered into a region of wonders, a place of magic. She freely gave herself up to it while, far out, the riding lights of anchored pleasure boats winked in the darkness. With lovers in them, Letty speculated in a sweep of daring, lying entwined, rocked by the waves.

They had almost reached the end of the Boardwalk. Garner took her hand, his thumb softly sliding along the edge of her palm. Almost as though it were her own body, Letty could feel his headlong energy slow down, change into something lingering, voluptuous, smoky with promise. Her pulse began to beat with a bumping, unsteady rhythm, a pulse inevitable and compelling, a pulse carrying her toward . . . what?

Garner remained silent, as though immersed in some colloquy with himself. Overhead, the soft drone and the blinking lights of the airplanes making for the Island Airport moved among the stars like moving stars themselves. From somewhere among the houses, a dog barked.

Letty's mind filled with images of Garner's mouth, laughing, speaking briefly in repose. His arm seemed to have tightened around her shoulders and she caught again that tang she had inhaled so secretly while dancing in his arms. With such a man on such a night in such a place! What could not fail to happen, even to Letty Smith . . . ?

She trembled with nameless anticipation. Their steps

brought them to a halt under a massive tree. Garner leaned against its trunk. Overhead, the stars glittered and the moon was embraced by a long, diaphanous hook of cloud.

"Enjoying yourself?" Garner asked softly, layers of meaning laced into his words.

"I've never had such a wonderful evening in my life!"

Letty spoke without reservation, her happiness rising to the surface like clear water welling up from a spring. The moonlight caught the fine planes of her face, the extent of her pleasure.

"Nor I, actually," Garner replied in a kind of surprise.

With a sharp, indrawn breath, he bent to kiss her.

The first hungry brush of his lips sent mad sensations ringing through Letty's flesh. She reacted with the shock of someone standing beside an unattended cannon which suddenly fires off. A raging sweetness poured through her. *Yes, yes,* her heart cried out. *This is what it's all about!*

Garner kissed her slowly at first, as though intent on tasting her, absorbing her essence. His fingers found her hair and tangled in the loosened tendrils. Very deep in his throat, he rumbled with pleasure as he pulled Letty to him so that her body was pressed against his, the tuxedo around her shoulders enfolding her like a second embrace and providing a tent of privacy. The moon hung above them with its crooked smile, not a little ironic. After all, had it not watched this scene played out myriads of times, through dozens of centuries, under its wise and knowing gaze?

Yet a banked fire cannot remain banked when fresh fuel is piled over the coals. The gentle, exploratory kisses grew more insistent until they ravaged Letty's neck and face. The dynamic man inside Garner, the man who reached for what he wanted and took it, came to life. Letty was whirled by the flamelike vitality of him, the strength, the power. They were far from people now, the darkness enveloping them,

the trees faintly rustling. This was a place where lovers
came deliberately, where the friendly shroud of the night
cloaked everything.

Letty did not even struggle against the rushing current.
Deeper and deeper they spiraled into passion. Then, without
warning, they were jolted by a small white beast that flung
itself eagerly against their ankles. Only Garner's swift re-
flexes saved Letty from stumbling backward over a tree
root. He tried to deflect the dog but it jumped at their knees
with a terrier's persistence, bent on overwhelming these
two strangers with a storm of wriggling affection.

"Stop, Scruff! Get away from there!"

The owner thudded out of the dimness, clad in a flapping
denim jacket, brandishing a leash thick enough to hold a
horse. She made an ineffectual dive for the animal's collar.
Scruff dodged her, all the while vibrating her tiny stump
of a tail. Scruff had a black head, pointed, inquisitive ears,
and she bounced continually as though composed of
springs.

"Little demon!" the owner sputtered, attempting a fresh
capture. "She just can't resist true love on the beach!"

With a lunge, she nabbed the miscreant, fought off an
assault of licks, and snapped on the leash. Then she hauled
the dog away, discreetly not looking back as she went.
Letty, emerging from her sensual rush, took a minute to
realize the resident was vanishing as quickly as she could,
supposing her dog had disturbed who knows what at this
unheard-of hour.

She probably thinks it's . . . scandalous! Mirth bubbled
in Letty's throat at the idea, the zany idea that she, Letty
Smith, could be scandalous. Oh, it was too wonderful for
words.

The swaying, romantic mood was broken. Garner came
to himself as a man swimming up from a deep depth, sud-

denly breaking into a brisk, sharp air. He actually shook himself, one hand running roughly through his hair in a now familiar gesture while the other retrieved the jacket which the dog had knocked down. Letty caught her toe. Garner steadied her. As Letty tipped back her head to continue the kiss, Garner's gaze raked her parted lips. His breath shuddered slightly.

"No more of that."

"Why?"

"You're tipsy."

"So!" Letty opened her eyes very wide, trying to focus on his wavery figure and make it stay still.

Garner only smiled crookedly and tried to slip the tux around Letty again. Letty pushed it away, full of tumbling heat. A mad, mad, perfectly glorious mood seized her. The sand, rippled by the footsteps of a thousand visitors, was now as abandoned as an Arabian dune.

"It's hot. I want to dive in the lake. I want to swim."

"Oh no!"

"Oh yes. Race you to the water. Catch me if you can."

She had shocked him at last. With a laugh, she sped away, losing her shoes, dashing barefoot over the soft sands, her skirt flying. She felt light as blown thistledown. She didn't even hear Garner pounding behind her until he made a flying leap just as she splashed into the water's edge.

"Yipes! It's wet," she squeaked as though this were some shattering new discovery. As much as Garner's grip, the cold assault of the waves brought her up short.

"It's Lake Ontario. What did you expect?" The aroused man of a few moments ago had disappeared into unsuspected boyishness.

"I expected," she cried, turning a half pirouette on her

toes, "to dive in like a seagull! To swim, swim away. Maybe all the way to Rochester!"

"I think you've managed to sop up enough of the lake already."

Garner bent to wring out the bottom of Letty's skirt, which was soggily dripping. He tied the material into a knot at her knees while Letty leaned on his shoulder.

"We'll just walk along the edge, then," Letty decided in sage compromise. "You have to take off your shoes too."

Garner looked nonplussed.

"Well, go on!" Letty urged, planting herself with no intention of moving until he complied.

With a little half hitch of his shoulder, Garner slipped off his polished footwear and slung them by the laces over his shoulder. The waves reached for their toes, making Letty gasp.

"I thought people only did this in commercials."

"What?"

"Walked barefoot along beaches in their evening clothes."

"Probably the people who wrote the commercials tried it themselves first. Just like you and me."

As they made their way, gulls rose indignantly and wheeled in the moonlight. Letty tripped again and Garner caught her. His eyes remained full of smoldering, unfinished promise. Without even thinking, Letty turned, hungry for more kisses. Garner bent briefly, then stopped.

"A man has only so many limits!" he grated under his breath.

Letty wasn't sure now whether there were not two of him, or three, but she wanted badly to kiss them all.

"Better hurry before another dog comes along. Why

would anybody walk a dog in the middle of the night anyway?''

"Because," Garner said, turning her around so she faced the eastern horizon, "it isn't night anymore. Look."

Far off there was the palest edge of pink along the rim of the lake. The stars had dimmed. More gulls, visible now, began to ride the air.

"Why . . . it's morning!" Letty turned to Garner as though the dawn were her own personal achievement. "I think we should celebrate!"

"You've had rather a lot to drink tonight, haven't you?"

"Um-hummmmm."

And I'm out with the most desirable man in all Toronto, she sang to herself through a shimmering haze. When Garner asked her how she felt, she considered the problem gravely. She failed to notice that they were no longer wading along the lake edge but angling across the sand toward the Boardwalk.

"I feel like singing."

Without warning, she burst into the first song that came to her mind, which was Grandpa Cotter's favorite from the Great War.

"Mademoiselle from Armentières, parlez-vous/Mademoiselle from Armentières, parlez-vous . . . Sing with me," she prodded Garner.

"I don't sing."

"Nonsense! Everybody sings. On a night like this, it would be . . . sacrilege not to!"

Encouragingly, Letty tugged at his elbow. She felt the muscles go tight, then suddenly loosen. All of a sudden, Garner broke into great gusts and snorts of laughter—freeing, easy laughter that shook his whole body.

"All right, Letty Smith, you win. What poor fellow could possibly have a chance against you!"

Garner's husky baritone obligingly joined in until they arrived at the car. Letty wanted to protest against going home, but the effort of singing seemed to have stolen her powers of argument. Therefore, she kept on singing, right until they turned into Culver Street, where Ricky Gambo's dump truck again blocked their passage. Letty opened the car door.

"Never mind getting past. We're there anyway."

She hopped out onto the sidewalk, unshod feet plopping softly on the cool cement. Garner sped round to grasp her as she began to weave in the rough direction of her house. He too was barefoot, his trousers rolled to his knees, exposing a rich expanse of hairy, sinewy leg. Letty burst into song again.

"Mademoiselle from Armentieres,

"Hasn't been kissed for forty years . . ."

Her unfocused gaze came back to Garner.

"That's not me anyway! Imagine writing a song like that about the poor mademoiselle. She should've sued."

The houses were all visible in the increasing dawn. Curtains twitched. Startled, sleep-puffed faces peered at the scene, but Letty didn't notice. Garner supported Letty up her walk and helped her open the door. For the briefest second, as she stood poised on the sill, Garner's lips lingered on hers, sending a frisson careening through her. She was certain her body was twinkling all over.

"Night night, Letty Smith," Garner whispered into her ear, and in a blink, he was gone. Letty floated into the living room by unknown means of locomotion. A jungle of feathery plants reached out to her in the semidarkness.

"Forty years!" Letty informed them. And collapsed straight into blissful oblivion on the couch.

Chapter Ten

Light, bringing reluctant consciousness, penetrated Letty's lids. She had been adrift, waltzing over acres of warm sand under a lopsided, dented gold moon. Now, a number of very unfamiliar, very uncomfortable physical realities impinged. Her skull seemed packed with gravel. Her tongue stuck to the roof of her mouth. When she stirred, darts jabbed behind her eyes.

"Uhhhh," she groaned.

"Oh, thank goodness! She's really going to wake up!"

Of course I'm going to wake up, Letty thought muzzily, recognizing her mother's voice. The fog in her brain made genuine wakefulness more of a challenge than she could manage.

Another groan. *Real world, please go away!*

"Letty Smith, you wake up!"

The command burst like shrapnel. Letty's eyes flew open. She half jumped away from the cushions on which she was lying. Mrs. Gambo, narrow-eyed, leaned forward from the kitchen chair upon which she had firmly planted her bulk. Ellen Smith occupied a chair similarly drawn up. Both stared at Letty and looked as though they had been staring for hours.

"Wha . . ." Letty gasped, then dropped her throbbing head back down like a shot duck. Daylight seared across her retinas. The light of a shamelessly sunny afternoon.

The living room! What was she doing in the living room?

Squinting downward, Letty saw herself sprawled out on the good blue couch and covered with a knitted afghan. Below the afghan, her feet stuck out, still clad in shredded, sand-encrusted pantyhose. She seemed to have a dress on too. Yes, the familiar yellow evening dress—only with the skirt in a very damp knot at her knees. And why was her audience eyeing her as though she were an escapee from the psychiatric ward?

"I called Gina over when I found you," Ellen explained tremulously. "You wouldn't wake up and . . . quite frankly, I was afraid you might be . . . ah, really sick!"

"Sick!" exploded Mrs. Gambo. "Ha! She got drunk, that's what's the matter with her. That man got her drunk and then he took her somewhere that wasn't no nice business dinner. Why is her skirt all wet? Why she got sand all over her feet and on the good couch too? Didn't I tell her, you don't go anywhere with any man you don't know who he is. You don't . . ."

Mrs. Gambo was swelling up into her most terrifying brick red. Letty floundered upward again.

"Oh no! No, Mrs. Gambo. It's all right, really. We just went for a walk on the beach."

"Beach? What beach? Nobody goes to a beach in the dark!"

"Oh yes they do."

Letty thought of the lovers dotted about in the shadowy park. Moonlight and Garner O'Neil's winelike kisses flooded back, momentarily blotting out the hangover. A soft, involuntary smile stole across Letty's face. She sank back with a sigh. Gina Gambo and Ellen Smith regarded each other in scandalized alarm. This was much worse than anticipated.

"What he do to you there?" Mrs. Gambo demanded heavily.

"He . . . oh, we talked, and we sang. There was so much moonlight it was almost like the daytime," murmured Letty from the depths of blissful recollection.

Even as she spoke, Garner again stood beside Letty, causing an immediate, thrilling shift in the pit of her stomach. I was drunk, she thought in sudden wonder. I loved every minute!

Drink was supposed to make you forget what you did while under the influence. Utter tripe! Everything, starting with Garner's kiss on the doorstep and rolling backwards, returned to Letty with luminous clarity. In waltz time, she skated away into the sunny memory.

Eventually, the silence in the room caused Letty to snap out of her altered state. Her mother and Mrs. Gambo still hovered starkly. Reality grew strong enough to chase up a flush on Letty's cheeks. Hurriedly, she plucked back the afghan.

"I better get up and . . . change."

The room went spinning. Letty's stomach threatened instant revolt. She leaned on one elbow until the danger receded.

"Did I really sleep on the couch all night?" she inquired shakily, only now beginning to grasp the oddity of it.

"Humph. Not much of the night. You and that man, you

wake everybody up singing in the street. Five in the morning, too.''

The melody lilted up in Letty's breast along with the pink edge of dawn just caressing the lake. Yes indeed, she had swayed shoeless up the sidewalk—singing at the top of her lungs.

Letty giggled. Then the giggle died in the first bloom of mortification. Drunk! She had come home drunk at five in the morning! How was she going to live that down?

This time the taste of Garner's kisses could not blot out Ellen's consternation or the glowering scrutiny of Mrs. Gambo. Letty hauled herself up and made for the stairs. In her own room, she slipped out of the dress and crawled gratefully into the private comfort of her own bed.

Eons later, to a sun low in the sky, Letty woke again. This time nothing in the room lurched when she opened her eyes. The house lay quiet and still, not even the television on. *Just wait,* the walls were saying, *until you get downstairs!*

Terribly thirsty, Letty drank more water in the bathroom and lifted her hand to her forehead. The face in the mirror gave her a shock with its wan greenish tinge and the ruins of her hairdo tumbled about her ears.

''Positively wasted!'' she exclaimed, appropriating young Suzy Cotter's favorite word.

Another giggle followed, so loud in the hushed house that Letty's hand flew to her mouth. Oh, she was in the queerest state, seesawing between her queasy physical condition and the unrepentant, cavorting joy in her heart. Sobriety returned at the prospect of facing her mother and Culver Street. Ellen, when Letty finally poked her head round the door, sat in sepulchral silence, knitting an afghan square.

''Mom . . .''

Ellen raised her hand in the air.

"You don't have to explain, dear. Everyone is entitled to go hog-wild once in their lives. I guess you've had your turn."

The expression "hog-wild" from the genteel lips of Ellen Smith made Letty start. The closer Letty came, the faster Ellen's needles clicked and the more she concentrated on her yarn. Why, she's flustered to the eyeballs, Letty realized. She hasn't a clue in the world what to do.

Letty busied herself making a cup of tea in the kitchen. There was no way around the fact. She had stayed out all night and come home inebriated. And with that racy bachelor, Garner O'Neil. Shocking!

She was ready to whoop aloud with glee!

When the tea was made, Letty felt bound to offer her mother a cup. As she brought it in, the needles slowed, then stopped altogether. Ellen peered at her daughter sideways. Her eyes were alive with unaccustomed animation.

"Was it all really . . . very exciting?"

Letty set the cup down wonderingly. Could that be . . . awe in her mother's voice? The tea steamed gently. All the plants seemed to stretch toward the center of the room, as fascinated as Ellen. Letty suddenly grinned.

"Oh it was, it was!"

And drawing up a hassock, she launched into the tale, telling all save the final, spinning saga of Garner's kisses.

"Well," breathed Mrs. Smith when Letty finished, "That is a story! You must remember it to tell your grandchildren!" Her eyes were as bright as if she had had the adventure herself.

At the word "grandchildren," an entire scenario unrolled in Letty's head—herself serene and plump in a flowered armchair with a row of little darlings about her knees—every last one a replica of Garner O'Neil!

The scene was so complete in every detail that Letty sobered abruptly. One freak date and she was weaving the man into her future—an exercise exactly on a par with scratching a boy's initials into one's desk in seventh grade.

The first edge of coolness punctured Letty's buoyant mood. A thin edge, to be sure, for Garner was still so near, his laughter so real, the pressure of his hands so alive on her body. Letty felt . . . familiar with Garner. Yes, that was the word. Familiar. Friendly. At ease. She expected, any moment, to hear his voice on the telephone or see that eccentric car slide down Culver Street, bringing all the children racing to look. Letty hungered to know about him, all about him, every detail, from his baby pictures to his shoe size.

She retreated to the porch to ruminate and pick up the newspaper. Too late, Letty realized that the moment her front door rattled, every neighbor sought a vantage point. Mrs. Garbo was scrubbing her front steps in ominous silence, pent-up lightning, a thunderstorm waiting to burst. Mrs. Packerson, on the other hand, matched the bemused expression on the jowly little pooch under her arm. The Sterns seemed to be asking themselves why they had never guessed what that quiet Letty Smith really had in her. From Grandpa Cotter's veranda chair came a sly, approving cackle. I should be reckless more often, Letty thought. They haven't been so stirred up since Art Beasley came back plastered all over with poison ivy from Camp Wigworman.

She handed the newspaper absently to her mother and went back into the kitchen to see to the teapot. She was interrupted by a yelp of delight from Ellen.

"Look, dear. Look! There's a picture of you in here!"

Incredulously, Letty saw herself smiling and dancing with Garner in the forefront of the glamorous crowd. The copy, thank the good stars above, only stated that Garner

O'Neil and Ms. Letty Smith were among the guests at one of the most successful galas ever. The joy of the dance flooded back, wiping out everything, even her hangover, in its wash. "That's me there!" she whispered, and stood gazing until her mother came up behind.

Monday morning, Letty walked into the Corral in a dream state compounded by a lack of sleep and the residue of Garner's kisses, which she had replayed over and over again in the night. When she entered the Corral, her heart did a skip. Today she really did have a whopper of an adventure to tell!

Unable to help herself, Letty regaled her friends with a dramatic account of her evening. The girls never took their eyes from her—and were only temporarily diverted by the splendors of the gala.

And they also watched closely as a flush of feeling quite new to her flowed under her skin, echoing those moments on the dance floor when she had whirled and dipped, so light, and oh so scrumptiously desirable. A smile appeared, one none of the Corral had ever seen on Letty's lips.

"But what happened afterward? Did he take you out anywhere? Did he try anything . . . ?"

Letty's tale had come to a screeching halt at the point when the last dance was over. She would have been grilled over coals before she mentioned the beach. Self-possession deserted her.

"Ah . . ."

Letty had trouble suppressing an idiotic grin. Her friends sat still and bit their bottom lips in what appeared to be open alarm.

"What?" Letty suddenly demanded, wondering why she wasn't being treated to all the shrieks and teasing and laughter the others stirred up when they told their tales. Melissa and Liz exchanged a glance.

"Oh Letty, it's about time you went for a loop over some man. We were getting worried about you. But . . . um, this one!"

"What's wrong with this one?" Letty wanted to know, feeling suddenly deeply protective toward Garner O'Neil.

Melissa, Liz, and Carol conferred silently again.

"Well . . . this," Melissa said, reaching under her desk.

She produced a magazine. In the magazine was an article about Toronto's eligible bachelors. Featured in a corner was a sexy photo of Garner O'Neil, Mr. Bachelor-of-the-Month.

The three watched Letty's astonishment silently, a tell-tale scarlet searing her earlobes. After a long moment, Letty closed the magazine and plopped it down firmly. She gulped a breath, like someone who is determined to pretend she has not just swallowed a burr.

"So?" she challenged, waiting for just one of them to state the obvious.

They didn't need to say it. A clear opinion of the sort of man who got chosen bachelor-of-the-month was written all over the three faces. Melissa sighed. "We just thought you ought to know," she said. Significantly, she did not retrieve the magazine from Letty.

Letty stuffed the magazine into her bottom drawer and found the stir created by her date was not merely a one-day wonder. A kind of subtle electricity established itself around Letty. Eyes which had ignored her now followed her as she passed, accompanied by whispers of speculation. A number of ailing plants were delivered personally. Even Mrs. Shelbourne strolled by to ask, with a brisk, knowing smile, whether Letty had had a good time at the gala.

Oh, it was all completely intoxicating, especially after Liz, Melissa, and Carol decided to be good sports and hide away their doubts.

Back on Culver Street, Letty attained a status somewhere between celebrity and Wild Woman of the Week. Who Garner O'Neil was, they had no idea, but the car had created more of an impression than a visit by a genuine prince of the blood. Grandpa Cotter sang a naughty version of "Mademoiselle from Armentieres" that hadn't been heard since the liberation of France. The Sterns and Mrs. Packerson suspended their feud long enough to discuss all the juicy details. Mrs. Gambo regrouped for three days, then went on the offensive.

"I write to my sister in Montreal. We find a nice boy for you. You don't have to run around with no maniacs!"

Oh yes, so many changes, both on the surface of Letty's life and in the deep secret part of her where she relived over and over again the magic night of the gala, the caresses on the beach. Changes quickly overshadowed by a single fact.

Garner didn't call.

Chapter Eleven

By the start of the third week, Liz was offering Letty a prime cinnamon bun which she and Melissa had refrained from devouring at break. They had taken to performing such small kindnesses without exactly saying to each other why. None of them knew what to do about a formerly reliable workmate who, by turns, either sat motionless in a dream-struck daze or attacked her tasks like a Roman soldier single-handedly subduing a barbarian horde.

At first, Melissa and the others, eternal optimists in spite of the magazine, decided Letty's state was quite droll. They would glance in her direction and wink indulgently at each other. As time drew on, their brows furrowed. None of them, of course, would be so foolish as to get shot down on a first date. However, since the victim was an innocent such as Letty and the man was Garner O'Neil, they were in perfect sympathy. Perhaps in such exceptional circumstances, they might not have been immune themselves.

"If only we could find a good, shriveled ivy plant or something, she might revive," Liz muttered. Yet, wouldn't you know it, even the supply of wretched plants dried up, as it did periodically. There wasn't so much as a sick geranium to be had from the whole fleet of mail carts.

Letty thanked her companions and bit into the bun without appetite. No cinnamon treat in the world could fill the hole inside her, but she didn't have the heart to refuse their eager offers. The bewildering welter of feelings, from euphoric joy to jolting despair which she had been subject to since meeting Garner O'Neil seemed to be flattening into this hollow, empty state. She struggled to accept the fact that Garner O'Neil would never show interest in her again.

In the hard light of day, Letty tried to balance the longing in her breast with a hardheaded practicality she had never known she possessed. Who do you think you are, the little voice inside her taunted, that a man like that is going to call you back? You never even got a return engagement after Elmer Gates took you to that guitar concert last February.

She had been an aberration of taste, a piece of self-indulgent whimsy on Garner's part. He'd tried his plant-rescuer and found her wanting, the way one dips impulsively into a bland-looking dish and finds it just as bland inside. Perhaps he'd found that after all he really preferred the fiery, exciting spice of other, bolder women who surely must flock around a bachelor-of-the-month.

Only—why did Garner have to be so convincing under that lopsided moon on the beach!

Her next step, the natural one, was resignation. Her evening with Garner was an evening of fantasy, a piece of magic dropped from the sky, a once-in-a-lifetime gift which she ought to gratefully cherish. To expect it to be repeated, to want more, was simply preposterous. What would Mr. Bachelor-of-the-Month want again with her?

And she might have been resigned if only . . . if only Garner hadn't left his kisses and his touch where every cell of her body remembered them—and longed for more!

Oh yes, retorted her own sharp logic, wasn't that the very essence of charm—the ability to make anyone, even a warty toad, feel fascinating while in its circle. Had she simply fallen, one more of dozens, victim to the tantalizing bait?

Letty swallowed some cinnamon bun and tried to squelch a small, hard knob of something very like anger. So what if the fairy dust had worn off and she found herself the same person she always was? Part of her, a good part of her, never expected to hear from Garner again. However, a bigger part of her did! Where did he get off, sampling her like a cake, then leaving her behind without so much as a nod!

Though Letty would have endured thumbscrews rather than tell her friends, she had actually resorted to flitting about the annex renovations to see whether Garner was there. She had finally encountered a foreman who had laughed breezily when Letty mentioned Garner O'Neil.

"Hey, doncha know, Garner's busier than two cats on a red-hot griddle. What with all the things he's got on the go and those foreigners chasing after him, can't say when we'll see him around here again. Look, wait till he checks in and I'll tell him you were asking . . ."

"Oh no, no!" Letty gulped in alarm. "I'm . . . it's not important. Please don't!"

Through with humiliating searches, Letty stuck her chin bravely into the air and headed back to the office. Luckily for her, the annual Culver Street fun fair and fund-raising bazaar was coming up, so Letty had plenty to occupy her.

As one of the stalwarts of the organizing committee, never mind the numerous responsibilities she would have during the actual event, Letty managed to work until late every evening and plop into bed worn out.

At work an expansion of business was going on. Fending off assorted depressing thoughts, Letty was just checking the rental agreements for a new high-rise on Eglinton when her telephone rang. Absentmindedly, Letty picked it up—and her heart skidded. She was instantly electrified by Garner's voice. He'd been thinking about her, he said. He had been rushed off his feet the past number of days. He was calling from Hong Kong.

"Hong Kong!"

Garner's voice faded in Letty's ears as she goggled over the fact. No one had ever phoned her personally long distance from outside the province, never mind Hong Kong. She could hear sounds of rush and crowds behind him intruding strongly over the line.

"I'm in a hotel lobby right now and I can hardly hear myself think. Look, the Rowens are flying out to Seattle tomorrow night, and they'd be happy to give you a lift on their corporate jet. Why don't you grab a bag and come along? You can stay with them, too, all right and proper. I'll meet you in Seattle Saturday and show you the town, and have you back in Toronto in time for work on Monday morning."

Casually hop a corporate jet to Seattle! Letty could barely take in what he was talking about. She had sucked in a breath and now found herself unable to release it.

"Letty . . . ?"

Garner might just as well have asked Letty to turn cartwheels over the moon.

"I . . . ah . . ."

"Here, just let me give you Rowen's number. Lucinda will be delighted to . . ."

"I can't!"

"Pardon?"

"I can't!" The whole idea was just too fantastic for Letty's mind to take in. All she could think of was the Culver Street fun fair, scheduled that weekend, of which she was a major cog. She clutched at the arm of her chair. "I've got . . . commitments this weekend."

"I want to see you, Letty."

Even over the distance, even over the clatter intruding on the line, Letty thought she heard a rough need in Garner's voice that sent her heart leaping to her throat. Temptation plucked at her.

"People are depending on me. There's no way I can cancel . . ."

In the end, she couldn't overcome her confoundment at the idea of skipping off across the continent on somebody's private plane. Garner, rushed by people and events, hung up disappointed. Letty's hand dropped from the receiver. She sat gazing at a pot of pencils looking rather as though she had just been shot between the eyes.

Only barely did Letty manage to keep the episode hidden from the sharp perceptions of her friends. Only barely did she manage to get through the rest of the day as her mind struggled with the stupendous fact that Garner hadn't forgotten her after all, that Garner called across a whole ocean just to invite her.

How could she possibly deal, she asked herself over the wild tumble of joy and regret in her bosom, with a man who phoned her from Hong Kong and expected her, on scarcely a day's notice, to step onto a private jet! And now that she had refused him—had she only confirmed in his mind how hopelessly limited and inexperienced she was?

Letty berated herself—and could not bring herself to imagine him phoning her again.

Nor could Letty possibly have imagined that, when she sped from work the following afternoon, Garner O'Neil would not be in Hong Kong, or even Seattle, but waiting for her in front of the building, patiently leaning against the fender of the Morgan.

"If the mountain won't come to Muhammad, then Muhammad must come to the mountain," he winked, opening the car door. "Hop in."

Letty stood dumbfounded, her pulse stuttering in unseemly bangs and thumps. She had been thinking of the hundred and one details that had to be attended to before the fun fair opened in the morning. Now she couldn't have been more confounded had an asteroid dropped from the sky and landed with a plop at her feet.

Pleasure beamed from Garner's face too, filling up the creases of his roguish smile, informing the tiny crinkles at the corners of those extraordinary pale eyes. His thighs were outlined in cotton pants bleached to the color of old bone. Over them a T-shirt seemed to hug every muscle outlined underneath. These were not the jeans and work shirt he wore when Letty had first met him or the stunning formality of the tuxedo he had worn to the gala, but some new incarnation which Letty did not recognize. Letty was too mindlessly happy to see him to notice that he also looked taut and sleepless and, above his freshly unfolded clothes, his hair seemed damp from some recent, rapid shower.

"I'm whisking you off to dinner," he informed her with a certainty that brooked no argument.

Without quite knowing how it happened, Letty found herself in the seat beside him. As though refreshed just by the sight of her, Garner vaulted into the driver's seat and they roared off into the traffic. Garner did nothing by halves, and that included driving.

"Where are we going?" Letty asked, managing finally to find her tongue.

"It's a surprise!"

The sense of danger drowned in another unreasoning surge of joy. He hadn't abandoned her. All her objections, questions, and thoughts, so grimly important an hour before, scattered like leaves on a merry autumn day. So much tossing and turning over just a mistake. Letty struggled madly for self-possession lest she turn into a pink neon beacon of delight.

Garner stepped on the gas, making Letty hang onto the door in the unaccustomed left-hand seat which every instinct told her ought to be the driver's side. Wherever they were going, Garner seemed impatient to get there. The rush of the car and Garner's strong hands guiding it had Letty quite unhinged. Against his mesmerizing nearness, she fought hard to remember the empty days that had just ticked past—and all the things she was supposed to be doing tonight to help set up the fun fair.

"You might have . . . warned me," she finally managed over the thousand beatings of hope and joy in her blood. Her asperity had no effect on Garner except to wring another half smile out of him. Today he was a high-powered engine humming near the top of its capacity. Vitality and drive sparked around him with almost frightening force and Letty, unused to this, regarded him warily.

"Then it wouldn't have been a surprise, would it? Anyway, I hardly had time, as I've just dashed into town with hardly an hour to spare."

The last small kernel of Letty's indignation melted away in a hot puddle when Garner cupped her hand in his.

The journey proved a short one. He pulled the car up at

Harborfront, Toronto's playground by the water, where part of the old harbor had been converted into theaters, restaurants, and an open-air park by the water. One of the old slips, arched over by a pretty bridge, was now a marina with rows of pleasure yachts bobbing at their moorings.

Lifting large bags from the boot of the car, Garner whisked Letty past the strolling pleasure seekers, past the long low marine store and straight down to the floating catwalks in the water below. Letty followed behind him on the precarious footing until, at the very end, he stepped onto a large, gleamingly white yacht tied up there.

"We shall dine upon the open water with only the seagulls for company. Won't that be fine."

Letty, who had never so much as set foot on a sailboat before, clambered aboard and sank down cautiously upon the polished wooden seat curving in the stern.

"But . . . what about the people who own this yacht? I mean . . . won't they . . ."

Realizing that she was making them sound like hijackers, Letty stopped. Garner unlocked the main hatch and shook his head.

"Don't think so. The yacht is mine—for the moment, anyway. This is where I live."

Letty's eyes must have popped wide. Garner got the hatch open and hefted his burdens easily inside.

"It's borrowed, actually. Just for while I'm in Toronto on the annex job. I get to live practically in the open air and come and go as I please. In a moment we'll be under way."

In a very sailorlike fashion, Letty thought, he proceeded to cast off the moorings and ease the boat out from the crowd of similar luxurious crafts bobbing all around. Shortly, they found themselves heading out into the harbor. Letty was so entranced by seeing Toronto Island, which sheltered the harbor, passing by, and the large ferry chugging over toward it, that the yacht was heading out of one of the harbor gaps before she jumped up in alarm.

"Mother," she cried, scarcely able to believe she had forgotten such a vital matter. "I have to tell her where I am!"

Before she could demand that Garner pull into shore somewhere, he nodded toward the interior of the boat.

"Cell phone in my cabin. Help yourself."

As Letty stood up, Garner regarded her simple mint green dress and inch heels quizzically.

"Better help yourself to some clothes, too. You're not exactly dressed for sailing. The locker under the porthole. Lots of T-shirts and shorts in there.

Apprehensively, Letty made her way in past the salon and the spotless galley to the cabin Garner indicated. The inside was tidy, and unfamiliarly nautical, yet Garner had put his stamp on it. His papers lay about, and the suit he must have peeled himself out of after the long flight hung from a hook against the wall. For a mad second, Letty wanted to press her cheek against it. Half afraid to touch anything, Letty found the phone and actually managed to dial up her mother.

"On a boat?" Ellen exclaimed incredulously.

"Yes. With Garner O'Neil. We're . . . ah, taking a short sail and we're going to have a picnic on the lake."

There was a silence at the end of the line during which Letty had another thought.

"The fun fair committee. I . . . forgot all about it. Oh dear . . ."

"Never you mind about the committee," Ellen put in with surprising firmness. "I'll deal with them. You enjoy yourself."

"Well, tell them I'll be there extra early in the morning.

I know how much there is to set up. Ida Cotter and I still have to organize the . . .''

''Letty, the fun fair won't collapse if you miss a meeting. I can tell Gina about it right now. I hear her on the porch.''

Letty rang off hurriedly lest Mrs. Gambo get her hands on the telephone. Then, balancing against the gentle roll of the hull, she got up the nerve to delve into the clothing locker. Immediately, the scent of Garner came to her, filling the cabin with his masculinity. Her hand quivered slightly as she stepped from her constricting dress into an orange T-shirt and a pair of blue shorts that she had to tie tightly at the waist. It was here, she thought, that he dressed for the gala. Somewhere, hidden behind one of the closed doors, hung the dark tux and the ruffled shirt she had danced against.

Letty emerged barefoot to where Garner gripped the wheel. At once, the warm afternoon air flowed over her and she expanded.

By now the boat had threaded the shipping channel between the Island and the mainland. As soon as they cleared it, Garner shut off the small motor and ran up the mainsail. The yacht immediately heeled in the breeze and leaped forward with an eager little shiver.

''It feels . . . almost alive,'' Letty said, swallowing her alarm about how swiftly they seemed to be going.

''A sailboat is said to be the closest to a living thing humans have been able to manufacture,'' Garner told her affably.

At the sight of the wind ruffling his dark hair, Letty suffered another spasm of longing. How she wanted to touch that hair. How she yearned to trace with her fingers that profile outlined so dashingly against the open horizon.

The yacht slipped easily along over the low waves until Toronto had receded to an impressive skyline with the needle of the CN Tower piercing the air against an unsettled sky. Only then did Garner haul down the sail and toss the anchor overboard.

"Perfect for dining at sea, don't you think?" He leaned back and worked his shoulders in a pleasurable stretch. "Man, it's great to get away from the rush and find a spot where a fellow can hear himself think."

The bags Garner had carried from the car proved to contain a splendid picnic spread of crusty bread, scrumptious cold cuts, ripe cheeses, fat grapes, and, of course, a bottle of lively red wine. Together, they laid it all out in the cockpit while the gulls wheeled speculatively overhead and the sultry early summer heat enveloped them.

Letty could scarcely eat for being next to Garner. She had fallen into the strangest state, intensely aware of how Garner threw his head back drinking in the sweet, lake-scented air all around them. When he massaged his neck, as though working at some inner tenseness, Letty wished she could do it for him.

His mouth is curly, Letty thought as they talked, like one of those naughty cherubs all grown up. The subject of kisses bobbed up in her mind and stayed there.

Nothing seemed more natural than that the two of them should be far out here, in this bobbing shell, with Toronto spread like a distant panorama before them. Unable to help herself, Letty was reminded of the riding lights she had seen that night from the beach and she thought of the lovers within.

Chapter Twelve

Aware of the madness of it, Letty did her best to shake off her fascination with the texture of Garner's skin and the way he took slow draughts of deep red wine from the glasses they had to guard from the rocking of the boat. After her experience with the gala, wine now tasted of danger to her—and thrilling possibilities.

"You didn't stop in Seattle," she said in an effort to strike up ordinary conversation.

"Since you weren't there, I skipped it . . . and came here."

Letty felt a flutter at the base of her throat. This was the thought she hadn't dared think. Nevertheless, it had trembled at the back of her mind ever since Garner had appeared outside Bandis Towers. It would also explain why he looked so rushed. Halfway across the world he had sped—for her!

No, impossible! That was far too crazy a supposition for

Letty Smith to believe. He had business, of course. But he had taken time out for this picnic.

Garner rubbed at the back of his neck again and stared off toward the city. Today he did not have the rollicking ease of the gala. Underneath his charm Letty picked up a keen undercurrent of restlessness.

"It can't be good for you," she admonished, "racing about like that. Don't you get jet lag? You really have to get enough sleep and eat properly if you're going to live like that."

Her tone, which was almost Mrs. Gambo's, made Garner look round with one brow lifted.

"Nobody's worried for a long time about me eating right," he told her with some bemusement. Then his voice dropped. "I like it."

A wave slapped the side of the boat lazily. Garner set down his wineglass with sudden abruptness.

"I better get used to dashing about. I was invited to Hong Kong by Adele Wong and cohorts. They're expanding into a worldwide development consortium—and they want me to join."

So that's what the undercurrent had been about. The preoccupation churning in Garner's head was almost visible. Business matters were all Greek to Letty, of course.

"Is it . . . something you want to do," she ventured, barely able to believe she was sitting on a yacht calmly discussing international consortiums.

The air, going still around them, seemed to have thickened. A pair of mallards winged their way toward the distant greenness of the Island. Garner stretched out one strong brown leg.

"It's very flattering to be invited. Adele Wong herself handled it all. She made a point of it. My company is very compact, easily mobile. An ideal acquisition for them, as a matter of fact—one more part of the range of services they want to be able to offer. There'd be work for me just about anywhere in the world I wanted to go.''

Without warning, Letty remembered the interested way Adele Wong had looked at Garner, the delicate, almost possessive precision when she had lightly touched his arm. Adele—who might contract Garner's company in order to acquire the man.

Something Letty didn't want to name twisted through her stomach.

''And in all those other places, would you live on boats too?''

Garner flung her a glance, saw she was perfectly serious, and burst into a gusty laugh.

''I might! Or have the use of houses. Or try out the most pleasant hotels.''

''Would you . . . know anybody there?'' Letty inquired, utterly unable to imagine such an existence.

''I would after I got there. There are always friendly people wherever you go.''

And friendly women, muttered the perverse little voice at the back of Letty's head. Would he take up with them as easily as he had taken up with her? Would they fall for him as rapidly as she had fallen for him? She pictured Fiji and Tahiti, lagoons so clear the pleasure yachts seemed afloat on air. Adele Wong would look so fetching in a white silk sarong while lazy palm fronds rustled along the shore. . . .

Oh drat that magazine that Liz and Carol had shown her! It was bad enough that the very idea of Garner globetrotting made the wine lose flavor in her mouth. Did she really, Letty asked herself, have to start scanning him for signs of bachelor-of-the-month behavior?

Firmly, Letty turned her mind away. She was out to enjoy a picnic on a boat, wasn't she—and not to disturb herself with fantasies she had no right to. It did not help that Garner, leaning back against the taffrail, had lapsed into silence, his face almost brooding, his thoughts a thousand miles away from the boat.

"The opportunity must be terrific," Letty plowed on doggedly.

"What?" Garner came back to the present and blinked. "Oh yes, it surely is. And a great compliment. People such as Adele Wong don't choose just anybody. The profit potential is enormous. I could expand all over the place—under the umbrella of the consortium, of course."

For a long moment the light of ambition flared in Garner's eyes as though he were entranced by possibilities Letty could not even imagine. His back straightened, his shoulders shifted, as though he were chafing to be up and off to the new horizons Adele Wong temptingly offered. Dimly, Letty understood that she was glimpsing the driving forces in him that must have made him so successful, so desirable to the Wongs.

Then Garner leaned back again and ran one hand through his hair in a way Letty already knew meant perplexity. There was something turbulent about him that his good humor barely kept hidden. Only natural, Letty supposed, faced with a proposition of such magnitude.

Letty shifted on the varnished wood beneath her. A seagull flapped down to the cabin roof, yellow eyes on the luscious glazed fruit tarts peeping from the pastry box.

"Things move fast for you, don't they?"

"Ha! The Wongs have given me just about a week to make up my mind." And at Letty's twitch of surprise, a raucous little sound issued from Garner's throat. "They're under pressures themselves, you know. Contracts waiting, clients to be satisfied. A window of opportunity, as Adele had already pointed out, can only stay open so long.''

Something dropped with a bump—or rather, a crash—inside Letty. If Garner joined up with the Wongs, how likely was it he would pass this way again?

The stern gave a fitful bob, spilling a few drops of wine over the edge of Letty's glass. The gulls in the air had begun swooping about in aimless, fitful patterns. There was a damp, humid scent to the lake which Letty supposed was natural this far out from shore.

''How can you just live out of a suitcase like that? Isn't it very . . . unsettled?''

It was as much of a protest as she dared make. For all she knew, dashing about the world without any burdens might be the most exciting sort of life Garner could imagine. Garner laughed, but again with that grating in it.

''It's true, a suitcase makes a very poor conversationalist—especially in the middle of the night. I ought to be used to it, though. It's how I've lived ever since I finished my first project. Flo takes care of my office space. I like to travel light, and I've never felt much need for any permanent base. I'll need one less than ever if I join the Wongs.''

''But your family . . .''

''None,'' he put in brashly. ''Not a relative on the planet. I'm free to flit wherever I please.''

''Oh.''

It was all Letty could manage. Her gaze fixed on Garner's bare ankles. He passed the pastry box. Letty took out one of the fruit tarts and put it on her napkin. Garner finished his in a few bites, as though he scarcely noticed it. Then he lounged back, lifting his glass almost in salute.

''And I flitted straight back to Letty Smith, didn't I? I never even thought about it. I just came.''

Letty glanced sharply to see if he was teasing but he was regarding her quite seriously, half surprised even at his own words. And even more surprised at the momentary lick of weariness surfacing in his own tone.

Letty struggled with a warm rush that had started up somewhere in the center of her chest. What could he mean? she asked herself wildly, her gaze veering away. Oh what could he mean by such a thing?

Garner wasn't going to explain, it seemed. When he got to his feet, Letty jumped up too. Between them, wordlessly, they cleared up and put things away together in the galley which, Letty discovered, was a marvel of well-planned organization. When they were finished, they were faced with what to do next.

Awareness of each other could not help but burgeon inside the enclosed space of the cabin. The sultriness over the lake seemed to heat the air around them, making their clothes stick to their bodies. Letty felt her own breath become very slow as the light coming in through the porthole outlined the long slope of Garner's shoulder and licked his thick curls with subtle shine. As they stepped outside again, Garner himself seemed to seek something to defuse the vibrations.

"Hey, how about a swim," he suggested, then laughed at the shock on Letty's face.

"Out here?" she croaked.

"Certainly out here. Just slide over the side of the boat and swim free in the open lake. Wonderful."

"I haven't got a . . . a bathing suit," Letty objected. She could not conceive of swimming without one.

"Jump in as you are. I have an infinite supply of dry shirts in the locker. What do you say?"

And before Letty could say anything, Garner dove head

first over the side of the stern and came up with a whoop, shaking sprays of lake water from his hair.

"Come on in. The water will make your hair stand on end."

Letty hovered by the rail. Then, possessed by the same recklessness that had struck her before in his presence, she sucked in a monstrous breath and flung herself in too.

The cold lake struck her in a jolting shock. She surfaced gasping. Garner, laughing, was beside her, one arm about her as she drew in air. His body moved against her in slow undulations. "Let's go," he called as soon as she had adjusted.

Together, they swam all the way around the boat to where the bow rose and fell gracefully above them. Letty reveled in the scary yet utterly exhilarating sense of being so far away from shore and so far above the bottom of the lake. It was like being launched on some voyage on which she would have only her own resources to sustain her. Yet Garner hovered beside her, a protective presence always near.

The magnetic tension that had been between them in the cabin now exploded into boisterous fun. They splashed each other, wallowed about, and shrieked with the abandon of cavorting holidayers knowing nobody else was around to hear.

Daringly, Letty dove down, deciding to slip under the very hull of the boat and come up on the other side. Unfortunately, she didn't reckon on the deep keel around which she barely scrambled in the murky greenness. Bumping against the side on the way up, she finally exploded to the surface, choking and sputtering. Disoriented, her head went under again just as a long form flashed beside her. Two arms grasped her and bore her up again. Garner bobbed with her, wet and shining as a seal. As Letty coughed furiously, a wave broke over their heads, inundating them with its chill. In a moment, Garner had them back to the stern.

"Had enough?"

Letty nodded vigorously, her teeth beginning to chatter. Garner boosted her up in front of him. They both flopped wetly into the cockpit, laughing and shivering at the same time. Lake Ontario, even at the height of summer, never exactly warmed up.

"Well, that was bracing, wasn't it!"

Garner plucked up a huge red towel and flung it round Letty's shoulders. After the water, the air felt warm and the towel wonderful. Letty mopped her eyes, then offered the loose half to Garner.

As he took the end of it, Letty found his eyes were frankly devouring her. Heat spiraled up from some deep place in her, hidden and alive, like the green, fecund heart of a jungle. She could not stop herself. Every sense, every nerve devoured Garner too. The square, solid muscles of his legs, the thick pelt of hair down his chest, the hollow of his collarbone all registered intimately upon her nerve ends. Suddenly there was nothing boyish, nothing playful about him.

One electric fraction passed between them. Then, with a groan as though he could not help himself, Garner dropped the towel and enfolded her in both his arms.

Letty felt her wet flesh sliding against Garner's. Garner's lips found the delicate skin next to Letty's earlobe. Letty responded with a stab of indrawn breath. A tremor passed through both of them. Garner's mouth found the corner of hers and began its honeyed work.

The towel fell unheeded to their feet as Garner's arms seemed more than warmth enough. Briefly, Letty caught a glimpse of the mast gleaming metallically above them before she shut her eyes, rocking with pure sensation. Garner was kissing her hungrily, tenderly, slowly, sending Letty beyond all thought. Time disappeared as Garner explored her eyelids and ran his hands down the graceful curve of her back.

When he pressed her tightly to him, Letty was overcome by a swift, violent hunger for him. It was like nothing she had ever experienced before. She flung her arms around his neck and began kissing him back with eager, fierce energy.

Garner groaned in the back of his throat and lifted his head away. His eyes were smoky with the same desire. He looked into Letty's face, then drew her to him again.

"I think we both know that something has happened between us, has been happening since we met," he whispered softly against Letty's ear. "Something that happens very rarely in a lifetime. We can't deny it, neither you nor I."

His nostrils were flared with the force of breath which he was trying to control. Surprise and certainty mixed roughly in his voice. Letty, enfolded against him, decided he was completely right. It didn't seem to matter whether they had known each other for five minutes or a hundred years. All that was irrelevant. What mattered was this immense thing only now making itself recognized—tremendous, electrifying, scary.

Letty tilted her head back, lost, lost in Garner's arms. Their soaking clothes seemed to have melded together. The flesh they covered telegraphed its heat just beneath. They began to kiss again, slowly sinking down onto the seat where they had eaten their picnic. Letty could feel Garner's heart beating wildly. The pleasure of his kisses gave her the sensation of spinning rudderless through space.

Suddenly, a sharp buck of the boat pitched them sideways, hard into the rail. Garner's head came up. He shook himself with difficulty from his sensual trance to look around him. At once, he straightened up and half let go of Letty.

The city skyline had completely disappeared. Black clouds had boiled up from the western horizon, flinging vast towers of vapor high into the sky. Gunmetal waves raced toward the boat, already edged with froth. Wind had begun to strike at the boat in nasty gusts, making the yacht pitch and career against the anchor. In the distance, sweeping columns of rain were racing across the lake, swallowing everything before them. Ominous flashes and rumbles sent Garner instantly to his feet.

''I let myself get distracted,'' he spluttered, fighting the thickness out of his voice. ''I suggest we get ourselves out of here as quickly as we can.''

Chapter Thirteen

A cold dash of spume, then raindrops big as pennies struck Letty as she struggled back from the fiery daze Garner had flung her into. He was already on his feet, balancing against the buck and slew of the yacht. Even as Letty looked behind her too, gusts of wind and rain struck in stinging whiplashes.

"Squalls can blow up in a blink on these lakes," Garner told Letty. "Grab the wheel and hold us steady before we get swamped by a big one."

Slapping control into Letty's astonished hands, Garner padded forward on swift bare feet. With no idea how to handle a boat, Letty gripped the spokes of the wheel in a frozen lock while the bow lurched and rolling waves began to slam into them broadside.

With only a thin hand rope between himself and the angry lake, Garner dodged forward through the maze of rigging to the bow. Letty went rigid with fright lest he be

119

pitched overboard by the lurching craft. Lashed by the rising squall, he battled with ropes until he managed to unfurl a small triangular sail in front. Immediately, the yacht steadied and swung with the wind like a weather vane. Surefooted, Garner made his way back over white decks now soaked by long tongues of spume.

"Never get back to the marina in this," he shouted over the howling set up in the rigging. "Just have to run before the wind with the storm jib until we find some decent shelter. You better go below out of this and get dry."

Garner's dark hair was flying in the wind that plastered his wet shirt against his ribs. The boat plunged and danced like a nervous thoroughbred, steadily assaulted by gray-black waves capped with long spills of foam. Garner took over the wheel but Letty refused to go.

"I'm staying with you," she cried. "Right here!"

Letty grabbed the railing so tightly she looked as though strong men could not pry her off. If she expected resistance from Garner, she didn't get it. He only paused, then suddenly laughed. Letty Smith seemed to have revealed yet another utterly unsuspected dimension to him.

"All right, so long I hook you into a safety harness."

That done, he took her into the crook of his arm as he steered the boat on its long race through the waves. The wind had increased with frightening swiftness, sending waves smashing over the bow and battering at the tough little jib. The yacht was already racing parallel to the shore. The city faded in and out of columns of cloud and rain, soon becoming invisible altogether.

"This is what the yacht was built for," Garner gritted cheerily to Letty's rain-washed face. "Let's enjoy it while we can."

Together, already drenched from their swim, they ran before the squall. Rain pelted them, cutting off all visibility save for an expanse of heaving water which lifted them up and up time and again, only to send them slewing forward into breaking walls of foam, which poured over the deck and away into the lake again.

Threatening as the dark welter all around was, Letty felt a gut-deep security as long as she was at Garner's side. So secure that, overcome with reckless impulse, she too began to take a crazy delight at facing down the blast.

The rain was so heavy that she felt rather than saw the boat swing sharply, wallow through dangerous swells, then shoot into a reach of water sheltered by trees from the rolling fury of the open lake. Immediately, Garner dropped both anchors and sped forward to take down the storm jib.

"Where are we?" Letty wanted to know when he slipped back. All she could make out through the rain were more trees and long swatches of marsh reed rippling and waving. The water raced about in agitated wavelets but bore no resemblance to the tumult they had just escaped. In the lowering gloom there was not a single light of any sort gleaming on the shore.

"Just a bay I know. We can sit out the weather here. Everything's shipshape, so let's get into the cabin and get dry."

They practically tumbled together through the companionway into the warm interior. Both were dripping wet, both were exhilarated by their adventure. Garner switched on the lights and swung Letty round to face him—a Letty no one at the Corral would have recognized.

"You look enchanting, with your hair like that and roses in your cheeks. Let me find you something dry to put on."

This time Letty emerged from Garner's cabin dressed in one of his sweatshirts and a pair of deck pants rolled at the ankles and knotted round her middle.

Garner, in fresh shorts, was naked to the waist and vigorously toweling his hair. Letty stopped, transfixed by the mat of dark hair down his chest. Something in the back of her knees went weak.

Garner caught her look. His look grew hooded. Once again the atmosphere began to grow charged.

"If I touch you now . . ."

Letty half closed her eyes, again swept up by a compelling impulse toward him. She wanted Garner to touch her. She wanted him to sweep her up. She wanted to drown in him.

Garner half bent, as if to brush her lips, only the rocking of the boat jogged her sideways, into the table behind her. Just beyond Garner, she caught a glimpse of the clock above the sink in the galley. Her eyes popped wide.

"Oh my gosh, look at the time. I'll have to call mother and let her know I'll be late."

"You might be all night," Garner informed her slowly, "if this weather doesn't let up."

He handed her the cellular phone, his bemused look saying he had never encountered anyone who had to call home so much.

Letty dialed her house and got no answer. Then she remembered this was Ellen's night to play euchre with the Gambos. There was no alternative but to try the Gambo number.

"You still with that man?" Gina Gambo demanded, not even considering the idea of letting Ellen talk on the phone.

With difficulty, Letty explained about the storm and having to take shelter in a bay. And that she didn't see how they could leave the bay in the immediate future.

"Ha! And maybe he make that boat run out of gas too. Don't matter where you are, you take a cab. We pay when you get home!"

Again the lunatic laugh plucked at Letty's throat.

"Mrs. Gambo, I can't exactly get up and walk across the water . . ."

"You walk where you have to. If you got a telephone to talk to me, you got a telephone to call a taxi. You want I give you the number?"

By the time Letty made her escape, she found Garner covered in a loose blue shirt and busy at the stove. He was brewing up a pot of hot chocolate.

"None of that microwave stuff," he declared as he poured out the finished product with a flourish. "Real chocolate and frothed milk. With a good dollop of brandy to warm us up. Here, try it."

The heated, dangerous moment of before the phone call seemed to have passed. There was something determinedly circumspect in Garner's face as if an old-fashioned courtesy had overtaken him. He did not, the glint of his eyes said, take advantage of ladies thrown by circumstance upon his hospitality for the night.

"Make yourself comfy."

They took their mugs and hunkered down at opposite ends of the long, thickly padded bench behind the salon table. Tired out by the rigors of the storm, they were glad to relax with only their bare feet brushing where their ankles overlapped. Letty moved with bemused slowness, as though trapped in some other medium than air. The chocolate, rich and scrumptious, helped erase Mrs. Gambo's forebodings.

Besides, everything had changed now that there was no leaving the boat. By now, Letty had sensed the unspoken agreement that had kicked in, an agreement not to touch each other or tempt the conflagration that would start. Instead, pleasantly languid, she and Garner savored a quiet companionship. Around them, the gently rocking boat became safe, warm, and enclosed as a womb.

When Letty felt the change in Garner, she let out a breath she hadn't even known she was holding. Over her longing, she was glad Garner wasn't kissing her. She had been badly shaken by the rush of passion that had almost drawn her helplessly into its vortex just before the storm. She wasn't ready for such a thing, had not even imagined such violence of feeling could exist. With the dark tones of Mrs. Gambo ringing in her ears and the grilling she faced on the morrow, she could not allow herself to toy with forces as strong as that.

"So," Garner murmured over a long sip of chocolate, "how do you get people to adopt all that vegetation that ends up on your desk at Bandis Towers?"

"Guile and persistence," Letty told him, with the most enchanting swoop of her fair lashes. "And, of course, some new green leaves on the skeleton to show it is really alive."

Garner laughed. Before Letty knew it, the two had fallen into amiable conversation. Garner told her about the scar on his chin from street hockey, explained how to deal with old plaster walls in a building, reminisced about how he had learned to sail while odd-jobbing at a marina in his youth. Letty found herself revealing her tenth-grade gym fiascoes, expressing her opinions on the ivory trade and divulging how to get a Brownie troop through a trip to the midway without lost children or casualties from the food. None of this seemed the least bit odd.

Letty allowed Garner into more small dramas of Culver Street, her face warming as she spoke of neighbors and friends she had known since earliest childhood. In the enclosed capsule of the boat it was easy to tell Garner about the stir he had created and with what interest they were all discussing him. Garner's surprise made her laugh.

"It's just the way it is in a neighborhood. We all watch out for each other and we're all mixed up in each other's lives. They take care of mother when I'm at work. I baby-sit on short notice and straighten out everyone's forms at income tax time. We all work keeping an eye on Grandpa Cotter.''

''The Cotters all live in that big brick house?''

''Right. The family descends straight from the early settlers on that land, you see. The house is actually the original farmhouse, so they still have those ancient maples in the yard. That's the trouble with new houses, they bulldoze everything to build them, then people have to wait twenty years for a decent tree.''

Garner paused, regarding Letty from where he leaned against the cushions behind him.

''You'd be planting from the day you moved in, I bet. If you had one of those new houses.''

''Of course. First thing would be a great mass of lilacs by the side door. Everybody always uses the side door. Every spring, the fragrance would be so delicious.'' In spite of herself, a dreamy, faraway look stole over Letty's features at the notion of a garden she herself could plan. ''Oh, and spirea, white cascades of it, spilling through the fences. Bridal veil, they used to call it. There'd have to be a trellis of climbing roses, yellow ones, because I loved them so as a child. And trees right away, so they'd be big enough in time for the children to climb . . .''

She fell suddenly silent, wishing she hadn't mentioned bridal veil spirea, and trying not to think of little O'Neils.

''Children have favorite roses?'' Garner asked with a kind of incredulity that threw his own unrooted childhood into unintentional starkness.

Letty nodded. ''Oh yes. We used to hide at the back of the garden and make up lists.''

Garner seemed to pause a long time. Something like a sigh, combined with a twitch of wryness, escaped him.

"In such a scheme of things, I'm not exactly your ideal man, am I?"

The question took Letty utterly by surprise. So many kinds of meaning were packed into it that she found herself without anything to say. Heat washed into her and out again before she found her tongue.

"You're just . . . you're not like any other man I've ever known. I never expected to know anyone like you," she managed with sudden, heartfelt force. It was, after all, joltingly true.

Garner flung his head back and stared toward one of the dark portholes.

"Who did you expect to meet?"

The word in Letty's mind was "marry." Something expanded awkwardly in her chest.

"Oh, I don't know." She tried to be casual. Then, because she too had her dreams, her face relaxed into gentleness. "I always imagined a quiet sort of fellow with a regular job, maybe at a plant or a bank. A hard worker, steady. We'd save up for things together, dollar by dollar. Once in a while we'd have a little business meeting and talk like serious folks about our long-term goals. Our kids would be perfectly ordinary, but we'd think they were marvels just the same. He'd come home tired and still coach little league. Yeah, and drive the team around in our beat-up van. And, of course," Letty added significantly, "he wouldn't mind living with my mother." Her mother was such a deeply, lovingly interwoven part of Letty's life that nothing could ever part the two.

When she stopped, Letty realized just what she had said and felt a twist of embarrassment about revealing such simple ambitions to a man who surely would think them laughable. Garner seemed very absorbed in his empty chocolate cup.

"What about the fellow who works in fits and starts, buys what he wants when he wants, and who'd think the children were all world-class geniuses? Suppose your mom got a personal nurse to look after her while her daughter scooted busily about the continent? Or the globe?"

Though merely a hypothetical question, Letty sensed at once it was all tangled up with Garner's ravishing kisses and the intentness flaring in his eyes.

He can't mean it! He can't be serious!

Now runaway panic galloped through Letty. She found herself unable to look at Garner, unable to lift her gaze from his shirt cuff or the strong, tanned articulation of his wrist protruding from it. A yawning void inside her yielded nothing to reply.

Garner caught the expression on Letty's face. A number of muscles worked along his jaw. Chaotic emotion skittered across his features before they composed themselves. After a heartbeat of silence, his regular self, keen and vital, re-emerged like a lost diver surfacing with a splash.

"Methinks the gentleman doth talk too much. So tell me," he murmured over the huskiness in his throat, "about that list of favorite flowers."

Letty, unable to cope with the unspoken issue that hung in the air between them, gratefully plunged back into pleasant triviality. By the time she got to the humble delights of sweet william and forget-me-nots, her eyelids drooped, as she grew sleepier and sleepier. Her last conscious memory before drifting off to sleep was of a blanket being tucked under her chin and, though perhaps it was a dream, of lips softly brushing her hair.

Chapter Fourteen

Letty woke with a start. The soft surface beneath her swayed and pale pink light illuminated the strange interior, causing a rush of scrambled confusion before she understood where she was. Not at home on Culver Street, that was for sure. The last thing Letty remembered was curling up among the cushions of the salon. Garner must have carried her to this bunk. Garner must have covered her with the light wool blanket that now enfolded her in cosy warmth.

Letty pressed her cheek against the blanket before muzzily realizing that the yacht no longer rocked as it had at anchor. It dipped with a rhythmic, purposeful motion. The cabin whispered with the sound of water rushing past the hull.

Rubbing sleep from her eyes, Letty sat up. The sight of her mint green dress, neatly folded where she had left it after changing yesterday, gave her an uncomfortable pause.

So she actually had spent the whole night alone on a boat with Garner O'Neil. Even though through no fault of her own, this was shocking behavior indeed for a Smith of Culver Street.

The rest of the boat also looked strange in the thin morning light. With Garner's things in evidence here and there, it had an odd, temporary, gypsylike atmosphere that added to the unsettled feel in Letty's stomach. Barefoot, she padded to the companionway opening, and peered cautiously out.

Overhead, a white sail snapped and Garner stood at the wheel. Beyond his shoulder, Letty glimpsed the shore, houses, trees, and all, rushing past at a steady rate. All trace of the storm had vanished. Under the dawn flushing the eastern sky, the lake glittered under a brisk breeze and a race of small, dashing clouds.

From her vantage point, Letty was able to watch Garner unobserved. The slanting light, coming from behind, threw his face into shadow. What movements he made were abrupt and efficient. With his hands on the wheel, his pale gaze ranging ahead, he looked lithe, restless, and intent, almost a stranger to Letty. Imagining himself alone, his features seemed keen-edged and taut, full of that preoccupied quality that had appeared only briefly at their meal last night.

Letty's gaze fell inevitably to the slant of his lips, bringing his heated kisses sweeping back. Suddenly, Letty was overcome by the graphic sense of how little she really knew this man. He looked almost a stranger—rakingly masculine, determinedly footloose, a bachelor who got written about in magazines. All the confident intimacy of the night before began to dissipate in the brisk morning air.

Letty's shape in the companionway finally drew Garner's

attention. His face changed immediately, shaking off the complicated brown study that had gripped it.

"Morning, sleepyhead," he called out. "Weather's cleared. We'll be back to the harbor in half an hour. Help yourself to coffee."

When Letty stepped out, the coolness struck sharply, waking her up fully. Clinging to the warmth of the coffee cup, she had no idea how charming she looked with her neat hair tousled and traces of sleep still in her gray eyes. She only knew that this unplanned night on the boat had somehow left her upset and disoriented. She was still wearing the rumpled sweatshirt she had slept in and could feel the aftertaste of wine at the back of her throat.

When Letty shivered, Garner slipped his free arm around her and drew her close against his warmth. They remained motionless together for some time, watching the bow slice elegantly through the waves. The yacht ran sweetly and swiftly under its white wing of sail. Letty felt her body fit naturally against Garner's. Yet even through the thick cotton of Garner's clothing, Letty could feel a tension in him. As the harbor gap loomed before them, the end of their voyage and the return to the everyday world, Garner suddenly gripped Letty closer.

"We don't have to turn into it," Garner broke out with a reckless tilt. "Have you ever thought of just running away? Going where you please, when you please? We could just take the boat and go—for the rest of the day, the rest of the week—the rest of our lives if we want. You could do it, Letty. Right now! With me!"

The last of the grogginess dropped from Letty's eyes. Her heart bumped unsteadily against her ribs. Was he teasing her to talk like that? Was he crazy?

When she flung round, the lean, timber wolf grin was there as Letty expected. But underneath was a kind of scraping urgency that caught at something deep in her solar plexus. Last night flooded back again, the surging desire as he had kissed her before the storm. For a blind second she thought how easy it would be just to turn the bow away from the city and plunge into the tantalizing unknown.

"Don't joke about such things," she blurted out, too taken aback to be other than direct.

Her head filled up with a jumbled, alluring vision of herself and Garner, their limbs tangled, their mouths seeking each other, tasting, laughing. By day there would be sunlight and the sweet wind. By night, the riding lights of the yacht would enclose them the same as the lights she had seen and wondered about that night on the Boardwalk.

Only then did Letty realize how seriously she was taking Garner's suggestion. A spurt of panic surged through her at the primitive, irrational power of the desire thrusting her toward him. Yes, she thought, it could hit that hard. Now she knew why people divulged nuclear secrets and had their backsides permanently tattooed with other people's names.

"What makes you think I'm joking?" Garner breathed in a voice full of mysteriously layered overtones. "For starters, let's have the rest of the day on the boat."

They were into the Eastern Gap now and it took all of Garner's attention to keep between the buoys and skirt the other craft making their way through. Then they were into the harbor where the sail had to come down and the motor started up. Garner performed all these tasks with deft skill. As he worked, he left the wheel in Letty's charge. Under her hands, she could feel every quiver of the hull as the very boat seemed to tug toward the open lake again. Garner's silent watchfulness told her he was but waiting for a word to turn them round again, back toward the freedom beyond the harbor gap.

Letty kept the bow straight, barely aware of the cool

metal against her palms. One part of her followed Garner's spare agility as he furled the billowing sail. Another part of her felt dazed, scarcely able to believe such a thing was happening, that such a man as Garner could want her, that she was tempted just to sail off with him.

And if she went off with him, there might be no turning back. . . .

Madness, insanity! the rational part of her cried. It would be tantamount to running off with a stranger met on a train. The strength of her own yearnings quite unnerved her. This sort of violent hunger was the kind of thing that happened to other people, not herself, the stuff of movies, not real life.

Yet here she was, gulping breath at the thought of Garner's lean cheek pressed against hers. And not all the cool, sober morning air in the province was going to change the wayward leanings of her heart.

The inner harbor was smooth and almost empty save for the Island ferries. Before Letty knew it, the yacht was gliding past the bright shops of the Terminal Building and into the marina. Wordlessly, Garner jockeyed the craft alongside the catwalk. When he had secured the mooring lines, he padded back from the bow and stepped, supple as a puma, down into the cockpit. One warm hand turned Letty to him. Lightly, he caressed her forehead with his lips.

''Well?'' he murmured, taking her head in his hands and running his fingers deep into her hair.

Instead of the persuasiveness she expected, Garner's look was direct and compelling. Something graven had crept into the lines about his mouth, something urgent that seemed, amazingly, to truly need her.

Again Letty pictured them, enclosed in the gently rocking capsule of the boat, with only each other, free and alone. She had no doubt of his seriousness—just the same as she had no explanation for it. Even as the fiery temptation tugged at her, Letty knew in her bones that if she went, her life would be, in some way she could not fathom, inalterably changed. She would not recover from rash action. There would be no going back.

As some early morning boaters clattered along the catwalk, Letty shook herself away from Garner's grip. Garner's hands fell to her shoulders.

"Look, this is important. Chuck whatever you have on for today and come along. We have to grab what time we can while we can...."

"Grab time?"

Suddenly Letty was appalled. Here was a man who lived on a boat, for heaven's sake, and flitted about the world with only a suitcase under his arm. She felt as though she were waking up, truly waking up, for the first time that morning. The very urgency that furrowed his brow set off alarms inside her. She was being pulled along by something she could not control—and perhaps he was too. If she went off with him, even for another day, she might end up so deeply entangled she wouldn't be able to extricate herself.

A seagull settled on the boom of the boat opposite and stared at her with cynical yellow eyes. Garner raised one of Letty's palms to his mouth. His warm breath almost undid her—until his watch flashed the time at her in bold black digits. The hundred responsibilities she was shirking tumbled down upon her.

"Oh dear. I have to get going. I'm going to be late setting up the fun fair."

Garner's head snapped up.

"The what?"

"The Culver Street fun fair. It's today and tomorrow. I run the organizing committee. I'm in charge of the money—which is all locked up in a box under my bed. Oh

and there's the food to see to and the booth mother is supposed to be minding. And I'm the only one who knows
where the prizes are for the pet show and the three-legged
races and the . . .''

''You turned down a trip to Seattle for a neighborhood
fun fair! This was your big commitment!''

Garner dropped Letty's fingers in open amazement.

Letty only saw that his brows had climbed right up his
forehead as though he had never heard of such a thing
before. For the past few weeks the fun fair had been a
central and consuming issue in her life. Now she understood how picayune it must sound to a man who dealt daily
with Rowens and Wongs. She stood up very straight despite
the dipping of the stern.

''We have one every year and the kids look forward to
it for months,'' she got out, gathering her dignity. Inside,
her stomach took another lurch at how alien Garner's real
life was to her quiet, ordered world.

Garner raked his fingers through his own windblown
hair.

''Letty, maybe I only have today free of business. Surely
there are plenty of competent people who can . . . deal with
the pet show prizes.''

The gap between them yawned at Letty. This neighborhood extravaganza, which had consumed Culver Street with
its preparations for weeks, was so small in Garner's view
that he could hardly see it.

Time to draw the line in the sand, as the saying went.

''There aren't,'' Letty told him with a brave lift of her
head.

And it was true. Letty was central to every bit of the
organizing. And she had flung herself into it more than ever
after the gala with Garner.

Garner clearly didn't believe it. His eyebrows, his

straight mouth, the skeptical tilt of his head all said so. Letty knew that if she didn't move soon, he would start kissing her hand again and she might be lost.

"I have to change. I'm late already."

Back inside the boat she fumbled into her green dress and stepped into the small, heeled pumps so unsuitable for catwalks.

"Letty . . ." Garner protested when she emerged again, but she only shook her head and scrambled up onto the floating walkway before he could touch her.

As she fled away, Letty realized what had been bothering her all along about the boat. No plants! Ridiculous, of course, the very idea of plants on a boat. Yet it was through the state of a person's plants that Letty customarily judged stability and character. No plants here meant a roving life without room for extras—such as a wife and children, a family who must be as carefully tended and nurtured as any geranium on a sunny window-sill.

I'm lucky, she told herself over her inner dismay, to get away before some real disaster happened.

Chapter Fifteen

By the time Letty arrived, out of breath, the park was a hive of activity. Letty barely had time to slip into her jeans before she was swept up into the whirl. Her adventure, she could see, was already common knowledge. Heads were together, discussing the matter. She received looks and winks and surprised examinations. Alice Beasley, between trips to stock the pie booth, said she'd heard Letty had been washed halfway to the States in a storm.

The blessed hustle of preparations, however, saved Letty from a much more direct grilling by her neighbors. And by some added mercy, Mrs. Gambo wasn't even there but off supervising the affairs of her sister-in-law's niece halfway across town who had chosen that morning to go into labor.

Letty herself was immediately besieged by people needing direction. There was the children's face-painting table to set up. The Wheel of Fortune game, rented for the weekend, needed tools to assemble, and a cash stake from the treasurer's box which Letty guarded. At the refreshment stand, a minor panic was underway. The wieners were still frozen hard as hockey sticks and someone had forgotten all about buying hot dog buns.

Letty plunged in, solving crises, making decisions right and left, finding scarcely a moment to brood about the scene that morning on the yacht. Ellen Smith, who had not been at home when Letty flew by, was comfortably seated in charge of the craft booth, which she had volunteered to mind all day. This was only fair since Ellen had knitted or crocheted most of the items stocking it. At the back, of course, there was a platoon of plants from Letty's convalescent collection, all in search of new homes.

"Well, you're back," Ellen exclaimed brightly when she finally spotted her daughter.

This was clearly an opening for Letty to recount her escapade. Letty got as far as the sudden squall, then was saved by two small Cotter tugging at her with urgent questions about the pet show set for that afternoon.

Despite the assorted hitches, the fun fair opened almost on time. People from all the surrounding streets began to pour in. The hot dogs thawed and sizzled on the grill, the Wheel of Fortune spun merrily, pots of homemade jam sold by the dozen, and children dashed about everywhere, dodging and squealing in high glee.

About an hour after the fair had started, Letty was lugging the end of a picnic table sideways so that a trio of elderly ladies could eat their pie in the shade. She failed to notice the sudden silence behind her until a voice vibrated almost at her ear.

"Perhaps I could help you with that," it suggested, even as Letty felt the other end of the table hefted up and shifted easily into place.

It was Garner, clad in blue jeans and looking raffishly appealing in the dappled shade.

"Reporting for duty," he told Letty with a wryness that belied their friction early that morning. "I've come to participate in the attractions of Culver Street."

Letty swallowed the blindly happy leap inside her at his appearance. As she settled the ladies, she felt a fierce protectiveness bristling at the back of her neck. Why was he really here, she asked herself, remembering all the things about Culver Street she had shared with him in the warm interior of the boat. Had he come as a sightseer in a world that was quaint to him, and amusing, but not important enough to cancel out a trip on a private jet?

"Don't you have . . . things to do?" Letty got out, meaning more momentous things than a local fun fair.

Garner shook his head, that half grin appearing again.

"Maybe I'm doing them. And I left the cell phone back on the boat. Now if you're working, I'm working. I'm yours to command. If you can't lick 'em, join 'em, as they say."

His blue polo shirt, open at the throat, hugged his chest and left his muscular arms bare. He leaned at his ease under the tree and glanced about with keen curiosity. To Letty, he was beginning to look familiar again, with his walnut brown hair riffling in the breeze and his single dimple showing. An impulse rose in her, combined with mischief and a sudden determination to toss Garner into the fun fair head first if that was what he really wanted.

"Well then, I sure can give you a job. We're run off our feet and we need all the volunteers we can get. Marlene needs help right away over there, at the face-painting table."

The look on Garner's face was worth it. After seeing

Letty was serious, he stalked, rather speechlessly, over to where Letty pointed. Marlene Pritt looked up in astonishment but rose gamely to the situation. Soon she had Garner in charge of a whole table of his own and up to his armpits in children clamoring for rabbit noses, cat whiskers, or petunias painted on their little faces. Let's see how long he lasts there, Letty thought to herself, as she dashed away to straighten out a mix-up over the pony rides.

When she had moved the two ponies, which a farmer and his daughter brought in every year, away from the fruit stand from which the ponies were taking bites, Letty sped back to the Wheel of Fortune to collect the excess winnings. After that she had to deal with one of the clowns who got an attack of the flu in the midst of a juggling act. Then, of course, the largest of their rented coffeemakers broke down, occasioning a scramble for the uncertain old clunker kept in the Beasley basement and used only when the bridge players met.

The pause occasioned by Garner's arrival had quickly given way to a fascinated buzz as everyone remotely connected with Cotter Street managed to go have a look at him. Eventually, even Letty herself found a moment to slip over, wondering if she would have to rescue Garner from a horde of shrieking youngsters and a goggle-eyed crowd.

When she arrived she found Garner had gotten over his perplexity and seemed to be having the time of his life. Using the same organizational skills he probably used to run his company, he had the children in lines, divided according to which kind of face they wanted. Those in the process of being done sat facing outward on the seat of the picnic table containing the paints. Rabbits, clowns, batmen, and sunflowers were being turned out at an astounding rate. Garner had paint on his shirt, his jeans, and his nose. His laugh boomed steadily. And from the giggles of his youthful customers, satisfaction was being delivered all round.

Garner spotted Letty and came over to the snow fence sectioning off his table.

"Still reporting for duty," he called cheerily. "How about you and I have some lunch?"

"No such thing as lunch for them that's doing the work," Letty chuckled. "Marlene will bring you a hot dog. I can use you later, though, when the pet show begins."

He looked so relaxed surrounded by the chaos of children that Letty suffered a vision of Garner surrounded by little O'Neils. As quickly as it came, the vision was gone. Embarrassed, Letty fled before anyone could suspect what had just popped into her mind.

Garner appeared at her side when the pet show began. Paint was also smeared across one cheek now and his fingers sported a rainbow of shades.

"Phew, I can hardly keep up with you," Garner told her, unwittingly adding another smudge to his jaw. "No wonder you couldn't be spared today. This is busier than running your own corporation."

Their eyes met. It was as close as they had come to sorting out the morning. Garner seemed about to say more when a horde of his youthful customers, now painted yellow and pink and green and purple, flocked around. Many of them had an animal in tow, ready for the next event on the agenda.

The pet show took all of Letty and Garner's energy to handle, with barking dogs, yowling cats, and, for a brief moment of panic, an escaped hamster in danger of being trampled by the crowd. Letty always loved the pet show best, and this year she was one of the judges. Delightedly, she got to hand out the prizes for best goofy trick, best pet/owner look-alike, fattest cat, and dog with the longest tail.

Leaving Garner in charge of herding the contestants safely out from underfoot, Letty dashed over to her mother's booth to see whether anything needed to be restocked. Behind her, the crowd seemed to have gone unnaturally still.

"Oh my good stars, Letty, Gina's cornered that man of yours," Ellen sputtered in a rush.

Mrs. Gambo had finally arrived and she had spotted Garner immediately. Her nostrils flared, her dark brows rushed into a knot, making her look thunderclouds. Letty knew all the signs and quaked.

"She's going to demand his intentions," Ellen whispered, craning her neck to see. "Maybe you better try to rescue him."

Gina Gambo, grim as a hanging judge, had planted herself squarely in Garner's path. Mrs. Stern and Mrs. Packerson flanked her stoutly. Grandpa Cotter scanned the periphery for machine gun nests.

Garner, who had been backed against the bake sale tent, looked swiftly as Letty hurried over.

"Mrs. Gambo," Letty cried. "What are you doing to him?"

Mrs. Gambo didn't lift her hot black gaze from Garner. Her face was mottled. Clearly, she was in a full state of war.

"You keep our Letty out all night! And now, my Rosa, she bring me this magazine." Mrs. Gambo waved part of the reason for her enraged condition. "Mr. Bachelor-for-the-Month, the writing says this big big wolf eats little lambs for dinner. We want to know what you mean with our Letty!"

So that's where it went, Letty thought disjointedly, knowing the magazine had vanished from under the cushions of the chair on the back porch.

"Mrs. Gambo, it's nobody's business how . . ."

"Business! Ha! Funny business, I think, trying to fool women with his fast talk and big noise. Look, he is even at it here!"

Mrs. Gambo waved the magazine again and turned suddenly upon Garner. "Where you get that crazy car anyway? I don't see no nice big honest callouses on your hand."

"I . . . revamp things and . . . make a profit," Garner offered, looking far too suspiciously humble. "And I did start with a hammer in my hand."

"Humph! I know all about that slick-handed business! The builders and the politicians, they scratch each other's backs and give each other what you call it, backkicks. Too mucha that going on in fancy offices everywhere around!"

"Mrs. Gambo! Don't do this."

Letty was actually about to tug at Mrs. Gambo's elbow when that lady suddenly swelled even larger, the better to loom at Garner and shake the offending magazine.

Garner bore the peculiar look of a man in the middle of choking, though whether from mirth or outrage, Letty couldn't tell.

"My nephew's wife's cousin, he drive delivery to that place you fix where Letty works. He don't see you there looking after everything. What kinda man don't check what comes off the truck, I ask. What kind of business can he run!"

"Well," Garner managed, getting control of himself, "business seems to be thriving despite me not looking into the delivery trucks. I can give you a full financial statement if you like."

"Maybe I read that," Mrs. Gambo muttered, unimpressed, "but I don't believe it much. You can write anything you want on a piece of paper."

"Mrs. Gambo, please stop! You don't need to do this!" cried Letty in a welter of embarrassment.

The Portuguese woman halted.

"Huh! Who's gonna do it if I don't. You mamma? She's a good mamma inside the house but how she gonna look after her girl when this kind of hungry fellow come grinning to the door? She can't, I say, so we gonna look after her girl for her."

Letty tugged at one massive arm but she had no more effect than a fly on an elephant. Mrs. Gambo rolled the magazine open to the jazzy bachelor spread again. It had a clutch of lovely women at the center, supposedly on the lookout for exciting men.

"Stop! I don't stop until I find out about these women who run after him. What kind of man tries to steal away our Letty? You make promises to these other women? You make promises to Letty? You break everything you say? You leave our Letty behind like a piece of old newspaper?"

Letty was appalled to hear her own deepest fears issuing from Mrs. Gambo's lips. Garner rose up as though blasted.

"I don't make promises I don't keep. I never promised any woman anything—"

The sentence broke. Garner's eyes flew to Letty's and caught her with a smoldering glance that made her heart stutter. She jerked at Mrs. Gambo with all her might. Mrs. Gambo turned with unhurried majesty.

"You better not," Mrs. Gambo declared with the finality of a woman who has made her point. She eyed Garner's excellent shirt as though it only confirmed his criminality in her mind. "You don't mess with our Letty or you be very sorry!"

"Abaaandon trenches!" cackled Grandpa Cotter, doing a smart about-face. "Foooorward! March!"

"Why should our Letty marry anyway," Mrs. Gambo flung over her shoulder as she went stamping past Garner.

"What she get for that but a lotta laundry and a big mustache tickling her neck in the night!"

The battered magazine stuck out from under Mrs. Gambo's arm like a general's baton. As Grandpa Cotter straightened to attention, Letty had a flash of the woman marshaling her motley platoon down Culver Street, marching staunchly on her swollen ankles. All in defense of one of her own.

Something caught in Letty's throat. Giving way to an unheard-of impulse, Letty stepped forward and caught her astonished neighbor in a hug. She let go of Mrs. Gambo's bulk. Briefly, the two stood staring, rattled at this evidence of the emotional high tides inside Letty. With one last sweeping glance, Mrs. Gambo lumbered off, her cohorts in tow, leaving Letty stranded with Garner. Logic told Letty she ought to apologize for the incident, but the rest of her rebelled at the idea.

"If you laugh, I'll throttle you myself," she warned spiritedly at the chase of expressions on Garner's face.

"I'm not laughing. Really, I'm not." He spread his hands in a gesture of surrender. "Actually, I'm impressed."

"Then why is your mouth twitching like that?"

"Because . . . well, that lady was certainly forceful. Maybe I should hire her myself. . . ."

Letty turned sharply away and began to walk. In an instant, Garner was beside her, his hand on her shoulder.

"I'm sorry, Letty. All I'm saying is . . . that I didn't understand how one could be cherished like that, by neighbors. You must really be important to them."

I am, Letty felt like saying. And I'm important to myself too. Her jaw firmed. She stood up tall.

"For god's sake, Letty," he gritted out, "all I'm trying to do is get your attention."

Those pale amber eyes transfixed her, eyes a girl could drown in so easily. Even deep breathing didn't help as Letty felt the familiar melting inside her.

"Look, let's get away by ourselves for a while as soon as the fair packs up for the evening."

All by itself, Letty's head bobbed as though it were agreeing. Before her mouth could utter anything that might incriminate her further, Letty sped back to her mother's booth, where she immediately forced three unsuspecting strangers in a row to take a philodendron home with them.

Chapter Sixteen

As the crowds thinned away and everyone was thinking of supper, Garner extricated Letty from piling empty cardboard boxes next to the Dumpster.

"Let the committees live without you for a while. Let's go off on our own and get a bite to eat."

Most of the fun fair was already closed up for the evening. In fact, Garner had done a good deal of the packing up himself, pitching in to clear out tents, set picnic tables back, carry coolers with leftover food, take down the snow fence on which children's art had been displayed.

Before Letty could object, he had whisked her into the car and they were gunning off down Culver Street, assorted residents peering after them until they were out of sight.

Letty, after a day of running about, collapsed gratefully into the seat despite the traffic rushing past so close to her side. Garner drove the car as though it were part of himself. In a flash, it seemed, they were downtown. And once through downtown, Letty realized they were making a detour into streets she didn't know. Seedy looking streets with winos propping up walls and alley cats darting down the twisting passageways where they had their homes. Garner appeared sunk in a pensive mood that wasn't broken until he pulled up beside a long expanse of brick wall. They had stopped under a sooty neon sign with one letter missing: J KE'S BILLIARDS. Old newspapers fluttered around the narrow door. Letty stepped from the car and stopped cold.

"It's a . . . pool hall!"

"Jake's a friend of mine. I'll show you how I misspent my youth."

Though Letty had rarely been in the vicinity of a pool hall in her life, she was familiar, via the Late Show, with their sinister innards. Crooks, gamblers, hard-boiled ladies of the night hung out in smoke-fogged corners. Maybe even a gorilla packing a .45.

"Won't they . . . I mean, isn't it dangerous?"

"Letty, have you been watching old movies?

Flags of color danced into Letty's cheeks. Chuckling softly, Garner drew her to the bottom of a dimly lit stair. His face brushed her hair.

"No use protesting," he growled, a melodramatic stage villain. "I intend to corrupt you and you cannot escape!"

In the narrow confines, Garner's lips sought the sensitive place at the side of Letty's temple. Letty responded with a stab of indrawn breath. A shudder passed through Garner. His mouth found hers and traveled along its softness. He moved his body over hers and she felt the wall at her back. Briefly, she caught a glimpse of a naked bulb swinging high above her head before she shut her eyes, rocking with sensation. Instantly, she felt the vortex tugging at her, ready to whirl her away. Warning rose in her midriff along with the emotions of early that morning. She managed to turn her head aside. Garner stopped abruptly. Drawing in a heavy breath, he took her hand and drew her after him up the long, worn stairs.

They pushed through the battered door on the landing. The combined odor of beer, stale cigarettes, and old wood struck Letty at once in the smoky den that would have done justice to any B movie. Caramel paint peeled off in blistered patches. A vista of pool tables stretched away, each under a harsh green metal shade suspended from a chain.

"Hungry?" Garner asked.

"Starved." Letty had hardly been off her feet all day. Garner led them straight across the creaky wooden floor to one of the three booths at the opposite side.

"Jake," he called out into some inner depths. "We need some sandwiches here."

A rotund man, dewlapped as a paste-colored bulldog, bald as a snooker ball, appeared wiping his hands on an apron. At the sight of Garner he broke into a vast grin and came together in a rough handshake.

"Garner, you old hound dog, is that you?"

"Long time no see, Jake. How the heck are you?"

"I'm all right. And you! The way you flit all over the country! Don't think I don't hear all about you on the grapevine."

Letty found herself inspected in detail by Jake.

"Well well!" he exclaimed, in much the same tones Flo had used at the gala.

"Well what?"

"Well, you lucky dog you," Jake turned from Garner to Letty, smiling through his many folds of skin. "Garner's never brought a lady to our . . . ah, establishment before. Not even when I used to have to kick him out for being underage. You never saw a more scrappy little mutt than fancy Mr. O'Neil was then."

As Jake spoke, Garner seemed to change subtly before Letty's eyes, taking on the air of a young Marlon Brando, shifting his shoulders, fitting into a roguish, slightly threatening environment. To Letty's questioning, fascinated look, Jake grew even more expansive.

"Didn't he tell you? This cocky young rooster started out on a pool hall. Wangled a mortgage, fixed it up, made his first packet."

Garner leaned back against a dusty upright, offering no comment. Jake barreled on with his story.

"Never had a hammer out of his hand until the last nail was in the last bit of door trim. And him nothing but calluses and sass from one end to the other!"

Letty met Garner's eyes for an interminable moment and caught a swift, dark flicker there. Why, he's giving me a gift, she thought, feeling a warm flood inside. He's trying to show me his roots too.

"I brought her here," Garner informed Jake, "because both of us are famished and there isn't a better sandwich in all Toronto than the ones you make."

"Never knew him when he wasn't famished," Jake winked at Letty. "Just give me a minute."

He vanished into the back again and shortly returned with two plates heaped massively. They truly were some of the best Letty had ever eaten—layers of thin, hot veal soaking in spicy sauce nestled in crusty bread that crunched so satisfyingly when bitten into. Letty demolished hers almost as quickly as Garner. The food filled her with a pleasant, comfortable glow that banished the weariness of dashing about the fun fair all day.

"Now," Garner told her when they had downed the last slivers of dill pickle and crumbs of bread, "I'm going to turn you into a pool shark. Let's take table number five."

He led Letty over the scuffed and pitted floor, past faded

hockey photos which fought for space with barely legible DO NOT SPIT signs. Rough-looking men hunched over a counter in one corner, drinking coffee and watching football on a large TV, the only item in the place that seemed to have been acquired after 1940. Still more deliciously sinister characters leaned over the tables making the balls crack loud as gunshots. Happy from ear to ear, Garner drank up Letty's reaction.

"I can tell it's just the sort of place your mother warned you about."

"My mother couldn't even *imagine* it!"

At the very thought of her mother's face, Letty burst into a giggle. A fine feeling was growing under her ribs, the simple pleasure of snatching, in spite of all, another evening by Garner's side.

"Good. Now for the nefarious game itself!"

They spent the next three hours absorbed in the game— and in each other. Pool, Letty discovered, had so many possibilities. Garner had to put his arms round to show her how to hold the cue. Their bodies bumped as they backed around the table, eyeing their next shot. Hands brushed, retrieving balls.

Garner melted even more into the environment around him, managing to look deliciously hard-boiled despite a smear of face paint he had missed on his chin. "Beginner's luck!" he yelped as Letty sank three balls and, at last, took a game away from him.

Yeah, Letty thought for a transported instant, beginner's luck all right. *Love* whispered something, completely without warning, in the region of her heart. As quickly as it spoke, it was gone, leaving Letty suddenly still-breathed, as after some deep sleep, straining to catch the sound that had jerked her awake.

When the game was done, they walked down the narrow

stairs again together, Garner's arm encircling Letty's waist.
It would have been so easy for Letty to just rest her head
sleepily upon Garner's shoulder and let herself hear night-
ingales singing. All evening, Letty had managed to blot out
the tension between herself and Garner. Now, still unsettled
by that strange, half-caught whisper within her, Letty
shifted away from Garner as they stepped out into the night.

"What is it?" Garner asked, supposing her still wrapped
up in her responsibilities. "Don't tell me there are fun fair
events still going tonight?"

"Well, the bingo game is."

"And you're supposed to be running it?"

"Oh no, I wouldn't dream of trying. That's Mrs.
Gambo's territory."

They reached the car, which was parked in a long
shadow. A lean orange cat removed itself from the hood to
a half-bald patch of grass, where it resumed the washing
of its paws. When Garner reached round to open Letty's
door for her, Letty paused, her gray eyes picking up re-
flections from the streetlight on the corner. A matter of
pressing import drove her to speak.

"The fun fair is running tomorrow too. Will you be coming?"

Garner shook his head.

"My time's up here. I'll have to fly out."

Cold reality burst into Letty's life, shattering the warm,
forgetful intimacy of the pool hall. A dozen emotions, all
of them unhappy, scrabbled inside her chest.

"Adele Wong?"

Adele wouldn't wait long for Garner's decision, they
both knew that. Letty pictured the city of Toronto utterly
bereft of Garner's presence and found it a throat-closing
prospect.

One of Garner's hands reached out to caress Letty's

cheek, halted in the air, and fell away. Garner leaned back on his heels and cursed softly under his breath.

"Sometimes the timing of life is about as lousy as it can be! If we'd met a year ago . . . if you knew me better . . ."

"Surely you want to join the Wongs!"

On other, less sweet lips, it would have sounded like an accusation. From Letty it was a kind of cry from one compelled to press a wound to see how much it hurt.

"It's the biggest thing that's ever been offered to me."

Letty knew, in the pit of her stomach, that he was going to go away and make his decision and there wasn't a thing in the world she could do about it. On the boat, she had seen the raw ambition flaring in his face.

Unable to help herself, she drew apart from him as though he were already entering a door through which she could not follow no matter how he beckoned. Whatever words she might have found lay frozen in her throat. She couldn't speak. She felt, all at once, quite colorless, all the fun of the evening drained away. What a fool she had been to float with such mindless euphoria back there at the pool table. Not when something precious, irretrievable, had been slipping, even then, from her grasp. Her moments with Garner were numbered. After tonight, when he dropped her off at Culver Street, she might not ever see him again.

"Letty . . ."

"I don't want to hear any more about it. Please, Garner. It's just . . . kinder to . . . leave things as they are. It's late. I need to go home."

And it was a need, as strong as that of a hunted fox for its den, to be safe in the shelter of her own bed.

Something beat for a moment at Garner's temple. He half leaned toward Letty as if bent on speaking anyway. Then, with a hard sigh, he finished opening her door. Moments later, they were speeding back with only the mournful whine of the tires for company.

Chapter Seventeen

"Goodness, Letty, have some coffee. From the bags under your eyes, you look as though you haven't had a wink of sleep!"

Dora Packerson paused to thrust a hot cardboard cup into Letty's hand. Letty, who was lining up the last of the chairs for the talent contest, took an obedient sip. Dora *tsked* in a motherly manner and hurried off to see about the curtain they had rigged on the makeshift outdoor stage.

Mrs. Packerson was right. Letty hadn't slept a minute. Instead, she had tossed and turned and punched at her pillow until the bedclothes were as knotted up as the wild turmoil of feelings tumbling inside her. It wasn't until she was truly alone that Letty realized just how much Garner O'Neil had taken her over. Like some jungle fever roaring out of nowhere, the thing had swept her up and would not set her down. She had no precedent for this, no suspicion that such a thing was possible. Was this what her mother had been talking about, she asked herself incredulously. Was this what mild Ellen Smith had meant when she insisted she hardly knew what was happening to her until the wedding ring was clapped on her finger?

Only with Garner, a man who lived like a homeless vagabond and didn't seem to want it any other way, the chances of a wedding ring, one that meant home and family and all the other ordinary things Letty's simple heart longed for, were just about nil.

There ought to be a law, Letty thought vehemently, that a girl's heart be in agreement with the rest of her. What an inconvenience, what a torment to have her emotions and, admit it, her body, panting after Garner while the rest of her clamored to flee over the horizon. Falling in love with Garner O'Neil, for that's what she finally had to admit was her problem, was like getting in a barrel to go over Niagara Falls. The ride might be thrilling, but the chances of survival were poor indeed.

To avoid her mother's sympathetic, inquiring glances, Letty flung herself back into the fun fair preparations practically at dawn. Everything had to be set up again and the food stands restocked, for they had sold enormous quantities the day before. As she worked, Letty tried, with little success, to tamp down the pangs inside her. Though she knew Garner would not be at the fun fair today, she could not help scanning the thickening crowds for some evidence of his broad shoulders and distinctive head. She contracted a little more inside each time one of the many youngsters who had been enthralled with him the day before asked about when he would come to paint their faces again.

Today was the day of children's games and the talent contest, which was the highlight of the festivities. At the center of the park, sections of wooden platform had been pushed together to make a temporary stage. All the chairs and benches around it quickly filled with expectant friends and family. Assorted contestants buzzed and fluttered behind the screens at the back. Letty was just allowing herself a minute of relaxation against a tree when Ida Cotter rushed up, face puckered with worry.

"What?" Letty asked.

"Oh, Grandpa's wandered off again. I can't ask the kids to go look because they're up next on stage. Suzy and Lennie have practiced their dance for weeks. They've been looking forward to it so and they'll just die if I'm not right up front egging them on. And if I let word out, the whole crowd will go off searching for Grandpa and spoil the show."

"I'll trot along and find him," Letty assured her neighbor. "You stay right here and clap for the kids. I know all the places he likes to go."

Letty sped off toward the houses, glad to be on the move, glad to have something to distract her from the gnawing knot inside. It was odd to find Culver Street so deserted even though she knew the entire population was in the park. She looked in all the porches and in the backyard lawn chairs where Grandpa Cotter had a habit of snoozing. She explored the alley where he liked to practice marching. She inspected the Beasley grape arbor where the old man retreated when he felt the need for camouflage. Grandpa Cotter was not in any of his accustomed spots.

Worried, Letty ranged right to the end of Cotter street. Then, reversing direction, she cut back across the far corner of the park to the little wooded ravine that made up its border. The deeper Grandpa Cotter went into his war memories, the more he had taken to wandering where he shouldn't.

Letty was just about to slip in among the trees when she

was halted by the crunch of twigs behind her and a sudden voice at her ear.

"Hey, where are you off to in such a hurry?"

Letty clapped a hand to her bosom to contain the startled bound within.

"Garner! You could give a person a heart attack coming up behind like that. I thought . . . I thought you had left Toronto."

Again, she could not prevent a mindless response of pleasure even though her face was wide-eyed with bewildered surprise at his unexpected appearance.

"I managed to book a later flight—so I could come back here. What are you doing wandering about in the trees?"

It took a moment for Letty to remember why. She blinked twice and got back to her current crisis.

"Looking for Grandpa Cotter." She pointed back toward the makeshift stage. "If I don't find him soon I'll have to recruit the audience over there for a mass search. It'll break the hearts of all the kids primed up for the talent contest."

"Does he favor ravines?" Garner asked, falling in at her side. "Mrs. Cotter spotted me as soon as I got here and sent me after you. She said she was afraid you were going to go into the hulk by yourself. What's the hulk?

"You'll see. Come on."

"Letty, I haven't got a lot of time. I want to talk. . . ."

"And I want to get Grandpa before the police do."

Letty didn't know why the idea of a talk frightened her, but it did. Before Garner could say any more, Letty veered suddenly to her right and seemed to vanish instantly from sight. Garner fought his way through the undergrowth after her.

"Wait, where are you going? You'll get lost in there."

"No way. I played every inch of it as a child."

To Garner's astonishment, Letty plunged straight down

into the little ravine. The forested bottom immediately banished the streets and gave the illusion of a totally green and natural world, as though the city all around were never there. Sunlight filtered softly down through the leaves. Wildflowers peeped among the tree roots and rich black earth. All Culver Street residents knew the place intimately from childhood.

Garner grasped Letty's arm and drew her round. Before she knew what was happening, he was kissing her. She was drawn into it for a moment, the fire inside her reigniting.

"I've missed you," Garner husked. "Even for an evening."

Letty struggled against the power of her own reactions and the urgency that seemed to grip Garner. She had another emergency on hand.

"Grandpa Cotter," she got out as she pulled away from Garner's grip.

Even in the diffuse sunlight, the marks of sleeplessness stamped her face, along with the dreadful conclusions she had been coming to during the night. As Garner opened his mouth to speak, Letty pivoted. Without looking behind her, Letty led the way up the opposite side of the ravine, finding footholds where there seemed to be none, vanishing so often Garner had to wonder whether she was part wood nymph. Lightly, easily, she found her way up the steep terrain and emerged at the bottom of a blistered wooden hoarding. The wood was weathered to a dirty gray and a chain link fence had been tacked up along the outside. Letty pulled a section of the chain link away from the post and pushed aside the boards on the other side. Supple as smoke, she slipped through the opening.

"Quick," she gestured as Garner paused, shrugged, and squeezed his bulk through the hole. As the last of him stuck, Letty grabbed his hand and gave him a stiff tug. He lurched on through and didn't let go of Letty.

They found themselves in a wilderness of rank weeds, tumbled concrete blocks, and the stubs of what might once have been a foundation sticking out of the side of the ravine. Letty led Garner along the rough earth at the bottom, then scrambled up until they were nearly at the brow of the slope. There she halted, peering carefully this way and that before stepping from the cover of the greenery.

"What is this place?" Garner demanded, pushing aside gigantic burdock leaves.

"Ssssh!"

Towing Garner behind her, Letty made a dash for a door gap and pulled him rapidly inside. Vast expanses of crumbling concrete stretched all around them, a warren of partial walls and weed-choked heaps of debris. Only when Letty had made sure they were out of view from the outside did she explain.

"Oh, this is the hulk. At least that's what Culver Street calls it. Years and years ago a developer tried to muscle an apartment building into the neighborhood. He got so cocksure about it that he started the foundation before he even had a permit. Well, Culver Street banded together and set up such a fuss at city hall! The permit was refused and the mess here had to be abandoned. It's been boarded up and rotting ever since."

"Culver Street stopped this!" Garner exclaimed, gazing around at the sheer size of the ruin.

"You bet!" The joy of the battle flashed again in Letty's eye. She had been only a kid at the time, but she remembered the excitement—and the alarm. "Culverites fought tooth and nail. Everybody knew that if this building ever got a permit through, then there'd be a whole row of monstrous apartment blocks up in no time—right on the site of

Culver Street. Our houses would have been swept away in their path.''

She told Garner about the heated meetings in one house after another, the fund-raising yard sales, the hours of putting up posters, the phone campaigns, the roused and resolute spirit of the street.

''My own mother telephoned until she almost had cauliflower ears. And you should have heard Mrs. Gambo ranting at city hall! No wonder that permit never got approved. Now we hope the whole thing will just rot into the ground and disappear.''

''So why, might I ask, have we sneaked into the remains today?''

Letty emitted a troubled sigh.

''Well, twice in the last year, Grandpa Cotter has been found in here and brought back by the police.''

''Why on earth would he come to such a ruin?''

''Look around you. The older Grandpa becomes, the more he gets carried away refighting the battles of his youth. His glory days, I guess they were. And did you ever see any place that looked more like a battlefield than this?''

Garner grunted, seeing her point.

''The owners pay the storekeeper across the street to keep watch,'' Letty went on. ''Even after all these years, they love nothing better than to nab someone from Culver Street and charge them with trespassing or mischief if they can. The Cotters can't afford fines. And if a social worker gets called in on Grandpa Cotter because his family can't keep tabs on him, then they might have to put him in a home. That would be the death of the old soldier for sure.''

''So we're in here looking for him?''

''Exactly. And being very careful—because we don't want to get arrested for trespassing ourselves.''

She had flattened herself against the weather-stained

cement behind her, her pink blouse looking like a splendid blossom amongst all the stands of weed.

"So how do we find him?" Garner wanted to know, ducking his head below the level of the broken edge of wall.

"Just be quiet and listen."

They remained still as statues but all they could hear was the rustle of the breeze and the sporadic roar of traffic. Letty had no idea how long Grandpa had been on the loose or even whether he was really anywhere near here. Worry knotted her stomach as she led Garner through one doorway, then another, without result.

Just as Letty was about to turn back, she half jumped out of her skin at a rasping shout from the front of the ruin.

"Ha! Dastardly Huns! Sniff about the perimeter, will you?"

Letty scrambled up on some broken blocks to see. The shout had been accompanied by a crunch of tires separating from the general traffic sound.

"I hope that's not what I think it is!"

"What?"

"Oh no! There's a police car pulling up across the road and Grandpa's spotted it. He doesn't take kindly to enemy uniforms. We've got to get him out of here!"

While the two policemen were crossing the road and struggling with the rusty gates of the site, Letty spotted Grandpa in a makeshift bunker where two half walls met. He was glaring belligerently toward the police car which was partially visible through the chain link.

"Sssssh," Letty whispered as the old man recognized her. "We've got to get back to our own lines."

The clang of the gate galvanized the old man. As soon as Grandpa Cotter realized they were on a stealth mission, he fell in instantly between the two. His small, shuffling steps were surprisingly swift. By the time the police officers managed to pry their way inside, Letty, Garner, and Grandpa were squeezing out through the broken hoarding at the back and vanishing into the leafy cover of the ravine. Hanging onto both his rescuers, Grandpa Cotter made his way to the bottom of the ravine and, with help, wheezed his way up the other side. Gaining the edge of the Culver Street park now, he spotted the crowd. Suzy Cotter was just going on stage.

"Huzzzam!" her great-grandfather crowed. " 'Bout time we had a show for the troops."

With that, he set out across the grass toward a very relieved Ida. Garner grasped Letty's arm and drew her back into the screen of the trees.

"Look, I have to fly out in an hour. The Sinclairs are hopping to the west coast again next weekend. I can meet you on my way to . . ."

"No, Garner. It's no use."

The cry seemed to come from Letty's heart and, not until the words were out of her mouth did she understand the true import of what had been happening inside her.

Garner's brows flew together.

"Have I developed warts or something?" he wanted to know. "Back on the boat it seemed to be a very different story."

The thing deep in Letty's heart howled despairingly.

"There's just not a lot of point in talking about it. I don't . . . we're too different." Stubborn pride made her still unable to mention Adele Wong for she couldn't have borne a single worldly comment about naïveté. "Our paths can't ever really meet."

Letty felt as though she had aged a decade since the day she had fallen off the swivel chair into Garner's arms. How did the issues between them get so intense, so weighty, so

. . . crucial! Her deepest instincts told her she had to break things off now. She had fallen too far too fast. To let it go further would only mean unspeakable heartbreak in the end.

"Letty . . ."

"Don't you see?" she all but wailed. "I could never live among the people you deal with every day. I'm not a Rosedale Smith or a Smith and Smith Investments Smith. I'm just an ordinary Culver Street Smith."

Garner went very still as his gaze fixed on the gentle outlines of Letty's face.

"I'd say," he said at last, "you were an extraordinary Smith. You've found your place in the world—something a great many people are never granted."

His words had a solemn ring, as though Garner had finally accepted what Letty had been trying to tell him. In spite of her best efforts, Letty felt a pulse pound visibly at the base of her throat and something inevitable clutch at her stomach.

"I'm just like you. I don't have a relative in the world—except mother. Culver Street is my family, I guess."

Even as she said it, Letty understood the deep truth of this. She had spent her life there, fitting in so snugly she had not even been aware of how deeply she and her mother were entrenched. She guessed what Garner was offering her—both now and yesterday on the boat. Another woman, an Adele Wong perhaps, would have been thrilled. All Letty could hear was the excruciating sound of roots being torn up.

Tendons and muscles showed for a moment in Garner's face, making him look remote, hawkish, stripped for action. Instantly, Letty felt she hardly knew him at all.

"Letty, I don't make promises I don't keep. That's why I'm not making any here. But I thought that you and I . . ."

"Yes," Letty cried, the admission torn out of her. "Yes,

it's true what you think. Don't you see. That's why this thing has to stop right now before it does any more damage. You can't just expect a person to break up her life . . . and . . . and . . .''

Letty stuttered to a halt, remembering too late that Garner hadn't actually asked her to do anything—other than sail off with him on that boat.

Garner ran a hand distractedly over his face and lapsed into silence. Where's that little voice you talked about, Letty demanded of him inwardly. That instant gut instinct which tells you which way to go?

The voice, apparently, had nothing to say—at least about her.

''I've only a few minutes before I have to get going or I'll miss my plane,'' Garner gritted out. ''I know how all this moving about is something new to you and . . .''

''Don't!'' Letty cried, feeling that if he pressed the matter she must clamp her hands over her ears.

Fearing his arguments, she turned away, her shoulders firmly set against this most captivating bachelor-of-the-month. And she held fast to her resolve with a fortitude, if she but knew it, that few women in the city could have mustered.

In the distance, Suzy Cotter came on stage to a roar of applause from all her relatives. A small yellow dog romped across the grass. Alice Beasley leaned over the counter of the hot dog stand, all the better to see Suzy. When the dance music struck up, it still could not cancel the silence behind Letty. For awful interminable moments, the tension pressed on her before it was broken by a sound. The sound of footsteps. When she glanced swiftly round, she saw only Garner's back—as he strode away from her toward his car.

Even the birds around her seemed to have lost their

voices. Letty's breath began to come in short, hard pants. He was going straight to Adele Wong.

Oh, oh, she wailed inside, even as Garner vanished into the street. *Oh, oh, what have I done!*

Chapter Eighteen

"*Linguine brava*. I take all day to make. You eat!"

Mrs. Gambo plopped the savory dish onto the kitchen table and stood over it. However, had she been holding a pistol, it would have had no effect upon Letty. Letty was beyond eating. She didn't see how food would ever play much part in her life again.

"Thanks, Mrs. Gambo. I'll try it later."

"You try now!"

Only fear that Mrs. Gambo might force some between her jaws made Letty pick up a forkful. Any gourmet would have been ecstatic. To Letty it was old sawdust.

A month since Garner had gone. A month without word!

"Our worlds can never meet," was what Letty had taken to whispering to herself like a mantra, especially when fending off the sympathy and puzzlement of Culver Street, which had taken more than a liking to Garner at the fun fair. Her encounter with love had left her as shell-shocked as though she had been through the Battle of Vimy Ridge with Grandpa Cotter. Yet though Letty knew that the siren song of Garner's presence, the knowledge of his very existence, might torment her for the rest of her life, it was better to suffer now and get it over with than be an appendage of a man who would, in the end, remain hopelessly out of her reach.

Mrs. Gambo watched Letty's pathetic efforts to eat. Ellen, from the other side of the table, flung out a confused and appealing glance to her neighbor. The Smiths had no experience at dealing with emotional upheavals and Ellen had been reduced to helpless silence days ago by the sight of a daughter tiptoeing about, white, silent, and mournful.

"He was such a . . . a stimulating young man too," Ellen whispered to her friend on the porch. "I thought for sure . . ." Her voice broke off sadly, as though remembering all the promise of the yellow dress—all the promise that had come to this.

"Stimulating!" Mrs. Gambo exploded vehemently. "I get him in my hands, I fix!"

At work, Letty's friend's waited, eyes alive with questions and interest. Letty could only shut her lips and fuss with her watering can exactly as though there wasn't a hard, pointy-edged lump sitting in the middle of her chest. When she tried to check the rent review figures for a twelve-storey high-rise they only skidded away, jumbled on the paper.

The weekend came, then another work week, a wheel of emptiness for Letty, a series of hollow, echoing days because they brought no hint of Garner.

Well what do you expect, the logical part of her sputtered. *You sent him packing!*

Yes, she had. And she'd meant it—almost. Logic wasn't a lot of good when she spent each day concealing a raging ache in her heart. It was hard to believe that Garner, persistent, determined Garner, could just drop away from her as though he had dropped off the edge of the earth. This silence wasn't like Garner, the man who wouldn't take no for an answer.

Not unless he decided the answer was no himself.

In the exhausting struggle between hopeless hope and grim resolution to put it all behind her, it was not comforting to discover things were just as she had suspected all along. Garner had proved himself a man of great verve and quick enthusiasm. An enthusiasm that had burnt spectacularly for a moment and then swiftly died.

"Oh does anybody ever know anybody," Letty lamented to herself at the end of another grinding day. "Was it all a fluke? A crazy, impossible, mismatched fluke? A man like that . . . and me!

For all her staunch efforts to buck up, Letty lost weight and color like a plant invisibly leached at the root. Mrs. Gambo sent over tempting dishes Letty could not touch. Frowns followed her down the street. Ellen rained worried, eloquent glances upon her daughter and finally, when they were sitting quietly together, got up the nerve to broach the subject.

"You've been knocked right off you feet by that man, haven't you dear?"

Letty emitted a raspy, ironic croak. She obviously hadn't been concealing very much.

"Heck no. I've just been sucked up by a tornado and spat out shredded on the other side. Hardly the same thing."

"If you want to talk about it . . ."

Letty leaped to her feet and went to stare blankly out of the window. With a sigh, Ellen returned to the rag rug she was hooking. Letty began to pace about, wanting to soak up the comfort of her familiar surroundings while at the same time fighting a wave of restlessness that crawled up her limbs and made it impossible to be still. She looked about her at the dear little house she had always lived in and felt, for the first time, how insufferably crowded it was, how the army of plants had taken over every corner and cranny and was almost in the beds at night. Her perceptions had been forever altered by contact with Garner's vastly larger scale of vision.

"Mom," she asked suddenly, "I've almost squeezed us onto the street with all these plants. How come you've never said anything?"

Ellen sighed and gave Letty a sidelong look.

"Well, it is a bit crowded, but I don't mind. I was afraid if I said anything, you might turn your attention to ailing pigeons or, heaven forbid, stray cats and homeless dogs."

Letty collapsed back onto the couch with a gulp of scratchy, woeful laughter.

"Oh mom," she gasped, "oh mom . . ."

And suddenly she was fighting back a storm of tears.

When the tears passed, the pain inside Letty flung her into a frenzied round of activity, tackling all the tasks which normally waited months, even years to get done. She dug out two cracked sections of the back walk and replaced them with patio tiles. She rented a steam cleaner and did all the rugs. She painted the porch railings. She washed all the windows, even the upstairs gable window which required she cling like a bat to the gutter nearby. All she wanted was to fall into bed in an exhausted slumber and sometimes, if she worked hard enough, she actually managed it.

On Saturday, she was managing, for the first time, to really sleep in. She snoozed very late, and woke up, finally, because there seemed to be music in the room. Though she blinked and peered around, the room proved exactly the same as when she had retired save for the sunshine slanting in. Her house plants stood in innocent green stillness. Her radio wasn't turned on. Yet there was definitely music. And a crowd too, if she judged by all the voices that seemed to be on the lawn. What's more, the music was very peculiar—all rousing martial melodies from the First World War.

Groggily, Letty passed to a front window, pulled back the greenery, and peered out. The entire neighborhood seemed to have congregated at the Cotter house. Besides the usual traffic congestion there were a couple of strange trucks parked at the curb, assorted building materials piled in their backs. What's more, barbecues were being set up in the park and what appeared to be massive quantities of food carried in.

Letty checked her memory. Goodness, it was Grandpa Cotter's birthday. Ninety-eight. How could she have forgotten?

Sighing at her own disorientation, Letty dashed through the shower, pulled on a shirt and shorts, and thrust her feet into her sandals. After all, she was the one who had been coaching Suzy Cotter and cohorts to sing "Over There," and others of Grandpa's favorites. Why hadn't anyone woken her up to help with the festivities?

Speaking of festivities, the party for Grandpa Cotter, if Letty remembered right, was to have been restrained out of deference to the man's great age. So what was all the riot about? And who, Letty wondered as she ducked round planks protruding from one of the trucks, had picked today to do home renovations?

Once in the Cotter backyard, she not only spotted Grandpa Cotter ensconced in state in a big armchair in the back porch, she found him serenaded by three live musicians who were at that moment swinging into a rendition of ''After the Ball.'' He had all his medals on and one rheumy eye cocked in case of sneak attack by any of those newfangled zeppelins.

Letty barely gave the musicians a glance. She was too busy staring at the heap of earth behind them and the great trench which assorted Gambos, including Ricky and Joe, were carving out of the Cotter's formerly tidy backyard.

Not only that, others were at work behind them, measuring and hammering and sawing, all the while referring to what looked like plans of some sort laid out on a sheet of plywood. A cement mixer stood nearby next to neatly piled bags of cement and a pile of sand for the mix. No one was enjoying this hive of activity more than Grandpa Cotter himself, who waved his cane gaily in time with the music.

As soon as Letty was noticed, the music stopped. The quiet was deafening. So quiet that all Letty could hear was her own agitated breathing and a trickle of pebbles falling into the trench. Everyone stopped talking and turned to look at her.

''What on earth . . . ?''

To her amazement, Garner O'Neil rose up from the excavation, naked to the waist, glistening with sweat and smudged with earth. His eyes met Letty's, direct and keen.

Letty could not have been more dumbfounded had a unicorn materialized out of the earth before her. For a few seconds, Letty's blood pumped madly before she caught herself.

''We're building a genuine wartime bunker for Grandpa,'' Ida Cotter put in excitedly at Letty's look of utter confusion. ''Grandpa can fight his battles right here at home and not wander off any more. And it's all a fabulous birthday present from Garner here!''

As proof, Ida flourished a sketch depicting an exact replica of a World War I trench and concrete bunker complete with all the insignia and furnishing Grandpa Cotter would recognize.

"Why . . . ?" Letty breathed, barely getting the words into the air. This was an enormous amount of trouble just for an old man with military delusions.

"He's doing it because he's got some great big announcement to make," young Jenny Beasley piped up, dancing from foot to foot. "He's been saving it up till you got out of bed. We're all dying to hear!"

"Yeah," added Suzy Cotter, not to be outdone. "And he's digging this big dirty hole because of you. Oh, it's so romantic I could faint!"

"Whatever he says, it better be good for our Letty," Gina Gambo warned, appearing at the back of the crowd wrapped in massive, foreboding dignity.

Ellen, seated not far from Grandpa Cotter, exhibited all the flushed concern of an alchemist watching a cauldron come to a critical boil. Letty felt her stomach lurch. Her neighbors were all grinning at her from ear to ear, hardly able to stand the suspense. It was clear what they thought the announcement would be.

Garner scrambled out of the trench, heart-stoppingly masculine, all sheened from hard work. Still gripping his shovel, he climbed halfway up the mountain of excavated soil so that everyone could see him.

"I've laid on food and music and the bunker for Grandpa Cotter because I want us all to have a fine time. It's only fitting, don't you think, that I throw a party to greet my new neighbors."

There was a small perplexed murmur and a good number of blank looks. This clearly wasn't what the street had been expecting.

"Because," Garner continued, "I am a new neighbor. I have just purchased the unfinished structure across the ravine, the one you all know as the hulk."

Whatever Garner had expected, it wasn't silence that was as shocked as a hammer blow. Tools clanked as they were dropped inside the trench. Letty felt a fracture open up inside her and her knees stiffen into knobs.

The hulk! There was only one reason a man such as Garner would purchase such a thing—he meant to ram the permits through and finish the monstrous block. Finish it backed by the bottomless funds of his new confederates, the Hong Kong consortium. They wouldn't stop at just one building, people like that. Oh no, they'd want three or four or five. The very clap of doom for Culver Street.

And she, Letty Smith, had been the one to show it to him, tell him about it, chatter idiotically about the row of other high-rises the original developer had planned. She had been the one, all unthinkingly, who had brought this ruin upon her beloved neighborhood!

Already, the faces of the old warriors who had fought so hard to stop the first project were turning stiff. Stricken eyes would fix on Letty. In a moment, when the news really penetrated, a buzz would start up, like a swarm of angry bees.

Letty could only stare back at Garner, her cheeks papery. Then the corners of her mouth jerked down. Before anybody could say a word to her, Letty was bolting from the Cotter yard, bolting home where she would be able to burst into tears.

Chapter Nineteen

Letty flew back along the narrow passage between the two houses where grass thrust through the aging walk and a neat niche sheltered the Smith garbage can. The sanctuary of the backyard, tiny as it was, had been turned into a private shelter by the lilac bushes and her father's hollyhocks, which thrust flower-laden spears as much as seven feet into the air. How could this have happened to her, Letty asked herself as she sank down into one of the ancient wooden lawn chairs almost hidden in the clumps of Shasta daisies. How could she have brought such a calamity down upon everyone?

"Letty?"

Letty half started to her feet again. She hadn't even heard Garner's footsteps. For a fraction she peered at the lovely muscles of his bare shoulders before the fury at his betrayal boiled up inside her.

"How could you go and do such a thing!" she all but

173

shouted at him. "How could you just use the information you got to . . . to buy the hulk and start up the trouble all over again. Oh, why couldn't you just leave us alone!"

The shock of Letty's flight was emblazoned on Garner's face. Little ropes of muscles stood out all around his jaw and turned his cheeks taut.

"What are you talking about?"

"How dare you come in here building a bunker for Grandpa Cotter and getting everybody working on it like fools and looking forward to a big barbecue afterward? How dare you when you plan to finish that apartment building and start tearing down our street again! Adele Wong and that big international consortium must have been really pleased with you, bringing such a good investment opportunity almost your first week. I bet you've got the permits for it tucked into your back pocket already, the way city hall is today!"

Tears were welling up good and proper now, streaming down her cheeks unheeded. The final straw that broke her restraint, the pity of it, was the realization that such a project couldn't be stopped a second time. Not with the government struggling out of a recession, trying to boost anything that might create jobs or yield tax revenue. Through the tears, Letty's gray eyes blazed at Garner in a most un-Smithlike manner.

"Permits? Certainly there'd be permits but . . ."

Words ground to a halt as comprehension finally penetrated Garner's horrified expression. All kinds of muscles relaxed and changed.

"Is that what you think?" he burst out. "That I'm going to keep on with the apartment project?"

"Well, aren't you?"

Mottled, angry red now stained the white of Letty's cheeks. Her jaw tightened and her bosom heaved defiantly.

"Certainly not. I'm going to have the ruins torn out so I can start all over. A modest row of town houses is what I have in mind."

Letty fell speechless, trying to digest this sudden change of direction. Some of the threat receded, though not her suspicions. The consortium could still build town houses all the way down Culver Street.

"Well, the housing market is picking up again. Town houses must be the new fad in lucrative investment."

"I hope so."

Over the peculiar softness of Garner's voice a screen door slammed in the distance. A dragonfly lit on a sweet william as the implications bloomed large and final in Letty's mind. This was a man who changed homes as casually as he got rid of last year's shirts. So he'd build the town houses, heaping upon her the torture of having him near while the project got going. Then it would be up up and away, as another enterprise beckoned, probably on some other continent.

Goodbye, love. Never could have worked anyway!

Letty dropped her head so that her hair swung forward, hiding the devastation in her face. She had to ask the next question, even though the abyss had opened in front of her, the yawning certainty of loss.

"You'll be leaving the boat then, moving on to some-place else?"

She was so painfully casual, plucking at a stem of grass, crushing its juices in her fingers. Her pulse thudded in slow, sickening waves.

"I hope so."

His words sent the twilight draining away over the rim of the horizon, draining, like her hopes, into nothingness. She couldn't look at Garner, nor swallow over the constric-tion in her throat. In the interminable silence, the dragonfly flew off and Garner traced a paint bubble on the arm of his chair.

"If I can find the right partner," he murmured, his voice shot through with a quiver, "that someplace will be home right here in this city."

Home! Whatever could Garner mean? He had always seemed utterly without any concept of home.

"I thought you already had a partner. Adele Wong won't be pleased at you living so far from Hong Kong!"

Letty found herself unable to look up at Garner, only at his battered construction boots caked with fresh earth. Remembering Adele Wong's fascinated look and delicate hand upon his arm, Letty was not prepared for the rueful sound he made, somewhere between a laugh and a sigh.

"Oh Letty, I pray you'll always be the same. I wasn't talking about a partner in business. I was talking about a partner in life."

Stupidly, Letty wondered whether Adele Wong was moving to Toronto bent on living with him. The tears that had been leaking from the corners of her eyes now dropped onto her wrist. She felt her hand slowly enclosed in Garner's two big ones. His thumb slid across the teardrops, leaving a smudge from the digging.

"When I spoke of an investment, I didn't mean an investment in the consortium. I meant an investment in living. I didn't join the Wong consortium, Letty. I turned all the globetrotting down. I intend for those houses I build to be just another part of Culver Street. And I want to make one of them my home!"

Letty could be forgiven if her mouth fell open and stayed open. Garner shifted still closer.

"Letty, it's as though I never knew what I really wanted until I saw you—and Culver Street. That day at the fun fair was one of the most educational days of my life. On the boat that morning, I couldn't believe anyone would have turned down a trip across the continent for a corny neighborhood get-together. Now I know why. Now I understand what it is to have roots. I want to put some roots down here.'' —

"But . . . to buy the hulk!''

Drastic, her tone implied, after only a couple of looks at an ordinary city street. Doubts, fears, and awareness of how little she really did know of Garner's life struck her. Humor plucked at the corner of Garner's mouth.

"I told you I was a man of quick decision. But when I make a decision, I also stick with it. When I was over there in Hong Kong being bombarded with the hard sell, I couldn't think of how much it would expand my company. All I could think about was a certain Letty Smith who was like balm to me on a warm summer night.''

Was she insane, or did the golden sunset clouds stop moving in the sky? He could be saying . . . he couldn't mean . . .

Letty felt Garner's energy crackling again, only leashed, this time, by some tremendous effort of will. He reached to lift her hand from the chair arm, cradling it tenderly in his own.

"I'm done with rushing about—and that includes matters of the heart. What I want, dear Letty, is a long and proper courtship under the eye of that fierce watchdog of yours, Mrs. Gambo. I want to chat up your mother and lounge about on porches and take you to ball games in the park. And after Mrs. Gambo is satisfied, and Culver Street is satisfied, and you're satisfied, I intend, Letty Smith,'' he finished very patiently, "to ask you to be my wife.''

It's odd that the human mind can blank out at such moments. All Letty could think was that she hadn't quite finished painting the porch and, when she did finish, when would it ever get painted again? A disjointed, twisting emotion welled up, filling her eyes with unshed tears. She felt panic and fear at the sheer madness of it all.

"We . . . talked about this before—sort of." Her voice was barely audible, even to herself. What had passed on the boat had been only broken-off innuendo.

Garner shifted his whole weight round to face her.

"Only now you're discussing it with a changed man. Look at me, Letty."

Letty, at last, lifted her head to gaze into his dear, ruffianly face. It seemed all sinews now, drawn tight by some intensity within. Could I do that to Garner O'Neil? Letty wondered, swallowing hard.

"We barely know each other," she heard herself protesting, thinking of how few, how very few, actually, were the times they had been together. Yet, since she'd met him in that annex, it felt as though a hundred years had passed.

"So tell me you don't know in your bones that you want me."

Garner caressed her palm with his thumb, the very slightest of motions, but enough to trigger waves of weakness and longing. *I must keep my head,* Letty thought desperately. *I must!*

"I knew I had to have you when I saw you rescuing that spider plant," Garner continued. "And I knew I had to have Culver Street when leaving it felt like walking from a warm room out into the freezing cold."

"It wasn't much of a plant."

But for such a little plant, such staggering results.

"It was enough. Enough to make me see I'd been living my life like a ball in a slot machine, zinging at the high scores. Like my dad. And his dad before him. Time to get off the roller coaster. Time to try solid ground for a change."

How could this ongoing festival of a man stop all his natural impulses? The rapid blinking of Letty's lashes gave away her disbelief. Garner leaned back into the mass of daisies encroaching on his chair.

"Actually, I kept thinking about plants. How I'd never owned any plants because I'd never be around long enough to look after them and they'd just die. They have to be looked after by someone, watched over, loved. That way they'd never be allowed to shrivel. That's the difference between a house and a home. I can buy all the houses I want—but only you, Letty, can make our house a home."

"Oh Garner . . ."

He held up his hands quickly.

"I know, I know. I see it written all over your face. You don't believe a restless bird like myself can ever settle down."

Letty didn't, couldn't say anything. She felt rather than saw him draw a shuddering breath.

"I was determined to live on that roller coaster and win. And I did win—for a while. But when Adele Wong and all the others were trying to woo me into their consortium, there I was, standing there thinking none of this was worth anything without Letty Smith."

He paused, the blood beating strongly in a vein at his temple. He licked his lips as though his mouth was dry.

"You can't raise a family on a roller coaster. A roller coaster is thrilling—but in the end, it isn't going anywhere."

Family! The word echoed through Letty with a yearning warmth. It all seemed so near. Was it also too good to be true?

Letty turned gray eyes upon him, swimming with thoughts she could barely express.

"Garner, what happens when some new chance pops up

and you're off after it like a hare in a windstorm? It's not in your nature to stay put.''

''Do you really have so little faith in my nature, Letty?''

The terrible yearning rose again, the instinct toward him, but still she sat immobile. Images spun in her head, and the panting words from the magazine article.

''There's a lifetime of chances for me just in Toronto,'' Garner added gravely. ''No need at all to hop from city to city, continent to continent. The Wongs and all they were going to expect of me finally made me realize that.''

Now Letty realized what had changed about Garner—and it wasn't just the earth all over him. He no longer had the look of a man burning rubber in the fast lane. The meteoric energy, the fascinating, unpredictable blaze inside had somehow changed into a fine, steady glow.

He must have been in overdrive ever since I met him, she thought. What she was seeing now was what Garner could be like when the great engine inside him smoothed out for a rest. Though outwardly agitated, he was also oddly at peace, like a man who has finally found his anchor and is now determined to secure it.

And I'm that anchor!

The knowledge made a vast, exploding pinwheel in Letty's soul.

She looked at him again, deeply considering. Could she, Letty Smith of Culver Street, hold such a man forever? Wouldn't he sometime, somewhere, be bound to turn his eyes to brighter butterflies?

Trust, trust yourself, part of her cried. But the rest of her asked the question.

''You don't exactly have a record of falling for office clerks.'' Letty dropped troubled lashes. ''I mean . . . there's so many others that are much more your type than me.

Didn't they bid like crazy for you at that auction? And the
magazine said . . .''

''That blasted magazine article! Do you want to know
the truth? It was all Flo's doing. She gave the magazine
the stuff to print. She put me up for the auction. Said she
had to do something to try and liven up my love life. Did
I want to end up some lonely old curmudgeon, she wanted
to know. Did I want to have my own private jet and nobody
to take on it but myself? Anyway,'' Garner put in softly,
''other women all have one overwhelming disadvantage
they can never overcome.''

Letty's gaze flew up, full of dreadful imaginings. Garner
began to kiss the tips of her fingers. If he didn't stop, she'd
be confounded utterly. Garner flung her a taut smile and
paused between her thumb and her forefinger.

''They're not you!''

His conviction tore at the last doubts in Letty's heart.
Garner retained his aura of infinite possibilities—only now
they were no longer frightening possibilities. Letty felt herself whirling toward him, helpless as a leaf on a swift, clear
stream. Frightened at the speed of it all, she grasped madly
at the last straws of objection.

''There's mother . . .''

''She'll live with us, of course.''

His kiss on Letty's palm made her gasp.

''And . . . all my plants. You'd have to sleep on the
dresser.''

Two more kisses rained down on Letty's knuckles.

''I've no intention of sleeping on your dresser. Not when
I'm in the same room with you!''

A honeyed shiver slid through Letty's abdomen. She began to realize what it would be like married to this man.

''Our house,'' he continued, ''would be right on the edge
of the ravine, with a glorious view of the Gambos. I intend

to build a huge greenhouse on the end. You can take in all the wrecks and orphans you like. Be a whole new career for you, running Toronto's first plant adoption agency.''

His lips found Letty's wrist and created deliberate havoc.

''You said one of Mrs. Gambo's daughters is getting married and they'll want a house. Mrs. Packerson is looking for a place to retire to and old Mr. Cotter needs more room to shout at the enemy in.''

''I don't see . . .''

''Next to ours, I'll build a pretty house, just the size Mrs. Gambo's daughter can afford. Then some apartments with all the conveniences for those too old to bother anymore with a house. And a playground, where all the children, ours included, get to play together and make it a real neighborhood. And a modest little shopping mall, of course, so we can buy our groceries.''

''One?'' Letty's eyes were starting to shine.

''Well, maybe if I see a promising bit of land, I might build a little something, just so we can live on the rent, mind you. And later . . . well, we'd see.''

Yes, he was ablaze with a new idea. But it was a manageable idea that would not run into heart attacks. Garner stopped kissing Letty's hand and became somber.

''My mother left my father,'' he said in a low voice, ''because of the way we lived. If I lose you, I'll be repeating his mistakes.''

His eyes betrayed a secret pain that must have haunted him. Now Letty's hand caressed his.

''She never did come back?''

''She's been dead for years.''

The dragonfly tried a marigold while, all around, Culver Street lay in an unnatural silence. No Cotter children tore down the streets, the Sterns were not sitting, like matched china pugs, on their front porch. Mrs. Packerson's dogs were evidently banished to the basement. Even the Gambo house sat in tomblike stillness. Never had Letty loved the place more. Never had she needed so much the support of all the people who seemed to be absorbed in other business.

"You're my other half," Garner said simply, and with enormous tenderness. "Without you, I'd go on careening through my life and never stop to see a sunset. I need roots. A home, a center, a heart. You're the most rooted person I know. Marry me, Letty, please!"

And I need you, Letty thought, for laughter and color and the sheer electric thrill of life.

Did she dare?

Letty hung, transfixed, mesmerized, trying to make her frozen system move. The tension stretched and stretched until she felt her every nerve would crack.

"When we're ready," Garner broke in, gripping her hand even tighter, "everyone will be in on planning the wedding. A bang-up reception in the park, don't you think, with dogs and kids and a guard of honor for Grandpa Cotter. We could honeymoon right in our own house, if you wanted, in amongst all the plants. . . ."

Letty didn't hear the Gambo kitchen window being thrown up, but she heard Mrs. Gambo.

"You take him!" Gina Gambo bellowed commandingly. "You're no gonna get rid of him no other way."

Letty leaped in her seat. Culver Street was not minding its own business after all. Ellen Smith peered anxiously from behind Mrs. Gambo. Cotter children choked on giggles behind the hedge. Mrs. Packerson and the Sterns had jammed themselves into the Sterns' front hall. Grandpa Cotter was being forcibly restrained from a military show. All had been quiet as posts to give her this chance with Garner.

Letty swung back to Garner, eyes sparkling.

"The vote seems to be in your favor."

Garner pulled her up from the lawn chair and enfolded her in a huge embrace. Somewhere, deep inside Letty, a mighty choir began to sing.

"You see," said Joe Gambo from his vantage point beside his wife, "I told you he's got the thunderclap. You can't do nothing about the thunderclap, only give in."

His hand found Gina Gambo's rump and pinched it outrageously. Letty and Garner were too much lost in another world to hear Gina's yelp of untranslatable Portuguese. Grandpa Cotter got loose at last and advanced, cane waving.

"Hooorah!" he shouted triumphantly. "God save the king!"